Tonja Drecker

DANCING LEMUR PRESS, L.L.C.
Pikeville, North Carolina
www.dancinglemurpress.com

Library of Congress Cataloging-in-Publication Data

Names: Drecker, Tonja, author.
Title: Music boxes / Tonja Drecker.
Description: Pikeville, North Carolina : Dancing Lemur Press, L.L.C., [2019]
    | Summary: When her family moves to New York so her younger
sister can
    attend Juilliard, twelve-year-old Lindsey finds solace performing in
    Madame Destinâee's exclusive midnight ballet shows until she
realizes that
    her fellow dancers are disappearing and Madame's music box
collection is
    growing.
Identifiers: LCCN 2018040062 (print) | LCCN 2018046523 (ebook) | ISBN
    9781939844576 (ebook) | ISBN 9781939844569 (pbk. : alk. paper)
Subjects: | CYAC: Sisters--Fiction. | Ballet dancing--Fiction. |
    Witches--Fiction. | Magic--Fiction. | Ability--Fiction. |
    Jealousy--Fiction.
Classification: LCC PZ7.1.D765 (ebook) | LCC PZ7.1.D765 Mu 2019
(print) | DDC
    [Fic]--dc23
LC record available at https://lccn.loc.gov/2018040062

To all those dreamers who do

Twenty-four stairs led up to the apartment, twenty-four final stairs. Lindsey squeezed her sleeping bag tight against her chest and stared at the staircase in front of her. Each step rose higher and higher, twisting in a never-ending spiral through the air. It seemed to snicker, as if daring her to go near it.

A mixture of dust and musty air filled her lungs as she took a deep breath. *Ugh.* She didn't want to be here. The house back in Nebraska was the only home she'd ever known—a big house with four bedrooms. Now, they were moving into an apartment in the middle of Manhattan, a small one with only two bedrooms. There wasn't even a balcony let alone a yard.

"Aren't these brick walls gorgeous? It's like taking a peek into New York history. Jacques d'Amboise was from this area, Washington Heights." The screech of Mom's shoes against the wet floor announced her coming up from behind.

Lindsey nodded and gazed at the brick walls. She was sure Jacques never had anything to do with these walls. He was an amazing ballet dancer and an even more awesome choreographer. Definitely not someone who would find plain brick walls exciting. Why Mom thought they were so pretty was beyond her. They were brown. Boring. Back on the farm in Nebraska, every room had been painted in a different color of the rainbow. The kitchen beamed yellow sunshine, the living room was caterpillar green, and Lindsey's room shone in misty blue to match the summer sky over the corn fields. Here, the walls were the color of squishy mud. Worms found mud fantastic.

Lindsey was not a worm.

Mom tugged her stocking cap over her head, making the black ends of her bobbed hair sink under a mushroom of pink fuzziness. "Go on upstairs while I grab the rest of the stuff from the car. Your father had to finish up some paperwork over at the warehouse, and I'm afraid your sister will get scared sitting up in the apartment all by herself." She tried to add a smile, but a yawn got in the way. With a pat to Lindsey's shoulder, she headed back outside.

Lindsey stared at the old staircase. Again. It hadn't disappeared while she wasn't looking, which was too bad. Taking a deep breath, she marched straight at it.

Creak. The first stair sent goose bumps up and down her arms.

Creak. The second could have come from a haunted house.

Sliding her heels together, she stretched her toes straight out to the sides.

"1st position!"

Skipping up to the next stair, she shifted her heels farther apart.

"2nd Position!"

Eight more stairs meant two rounds through all five ballet positions. The first landing was perfect for a *pirouette*. She planted her legs, threw one arm up into the air, and spun with the sleeping bag clutched to her chest. Around and around and around...

Her boot stuck like old bubblegum, and she went flying against the railing. At first her breath caught, but then a giggle slipped out. Staring past the banister, she gazed up at the stairs above. Five floors shot upwards high and tall.

"Hello!" Her voice echoed, and she couldn't help but smile. "Hello! Hello!" she called again, and her voice echoed back. She had to tell Bridget. She'd love it.

Squeak. The sound raked from behind—loud and long.

Clunk.

Swallowing hard, Lindsey gripped the sleeping bag as a shield and spun around.

The door on the left, Apartment 2A, opened. The smell of moth balls and lemony cleaner poured from inside. An old woman appeared from the shadows beyond the door. Ringlets of tight gray hair piled into a wobbly mound on top of her head.

Each of her movements carried the moan of ten thousand years. The woman shoved a folding chair smack dab in the middle of the doorway and plopped down onto it. The aluminum groaned under the weight of her over-sized backside as she folded her arms across her chest and glared.

"Hello." Lindsey cranked a friendly smile, one that hopefully fit introductions to new neighbors...even the kind that gave her the creeps. "I'm Lindsey. We're moving in upstairs."

The woman's lips cranked from one side to the other, and the mole under her nose wiggled like a fat bug. She drew in a rattling breathe and held it.

One...

Two...

"Don't play on the stairs!"

Lindsey yelped and bolted up the next flight, stumbling as her feet tried to keep up with the rest of her. Her boots screeched when she hit the next landing and skidded through the open door to the right.

"Bridget?" The words stuck in her throat. "Bridget?" she screamed louder.

Nobody answered. Emptiness settled in.

Fighting a shiver, Lindsey stared at the living room. White paint beckoned from every side, except for the far wall. That one was brick, the kind her mom liked so much. A row of windows stretched across one of the other walls from ceiling to floor, which might invite the sun in if it weren't so cloudy. But it was. Super dreary and gray.

Off in the corner, a kitchen stood guarded by a breakfast island. A short hallway with three doors shot off to the right. The door at the end of the hall was open, displaying a bathtub. That left the two other doors: one to the left, and one to the right.

"Bridget?" she repeated, sliding toward the hallway.

An off-pitched tone sang from behind the door on the right.

When Lindsey opened it, she found walls striped white and pink, carrying as much excitement as a paled candy cane.

Bridget sat cross-legged in the middle of the bare wooden floor. She brought the violin down from her shoulder and perched it straight up between her legs. She rested her chin on the end of the scroll, making her cheeks puff out like a big bull frog.

Lindsey dropped her sleeping bag to the floor and slumped down on top of it. Her heart still thundered in her ears, and she had to stuff her hands under her thighs to keep them from shaking. "Did you see the woman downstairs?"

Bridget shook her head, making her pigtails flop against her cheeks. "Nope."

"Good. You don't want to. Trust me. She's a witch."

Bridget's chocolate eyes widened. "A real witch? Did she cast a spell on you?"

"No, not that kind of witch. I meant she's mean. Cranky." Lindsey started to roll her eyes but stopped. Bridget was smart when it came to school and especially her violin, but she was more gullible than most eight-year-olds. Getting to her knees, Lindsey untied the sleeping bag and rolled it open across the floor.

"Don't worry. I won't let her turn you into a toad."

Bridget pursed her lips. "We can sneak downstairs and steal her broomstick."

And fly all the way back to Nebraska. Lindsey picked at the end of the zipper, wondering if any of her friends back home would let her move in with them. But Mom and Dad wouldn't approve of that. Not in a thousand years.

"Bridget, I don't hear the violin." Mom's voice came from somewhere past the apartment door.

Bridget sighed and shoved her violin under her chin. "Maybe the witch could cast a spell to make my violin practice itself." A second later, music filled the room.

Lindsey stretched out across her sleeping bag and stared at the light bulb bobbing down from a bare wire sticking out of the ceiling. It hung there, dusty and alone.

Everything the McKay family owned was stuffed in the back of a moving truck battling its way through a blizzard somewhere on the other side of the country. All Lindsey had was one super-small suitcase with a couple of sweaters, jeans, socks, and underwear. And her music box. Mom insisted she pack it in her suitcase for fear it might be damaged in the moving truck.

Lindsey had to take out her ballet outfit to make it fit. The trade was anything but fair, but there was no arguing with Mom.

Shaking off a sudden chill, Lindsey dug the music box out of her suitcase and balanced it on her knee. It had been a present from Grandma for her twelfth birthday—a handmade original from the famous toymaker Jeannot Broussard. Being a collector's item, it was expensive, too. Mostly because the toymaker had disappeared without a trace after his sister's ballet performance in Paris. Completely vanished. All that was ever found of him was a pile of clothes in the center of her dressing room with a big, red apple in the middle of his shirt collar where his head would have been.

The lid of the music box squeaked as Lindsey lifted it. The tiny ballerina inside spun on her pedestal. Her yellow tutu flared out like rays of sunshine. Her smile beamed. Her posture was perfect. Lindsey closed her eyes and pictured herself on a stage. The music playing...the crowd applauding...

"I'm sorry." Bridget held her violin half-kilter between her legs and chin.

Lindsey sniffed and quickly rubbed away tears she didn't know she had. "Sorry for what?"

"For everything. I know you're sad, and I know it's my fault." Bridget's eyes shimmered.

Hopefully not with real tears. Lindsey could stand almost anything but not when Bridget cried.

"Don't be a goofball. Nothing's your fault. You're amazing! How many people get to say that their little sister will be one of the best violinists in the world and mean it?"

Bridget pushed her legs out straight, making the bells on her Christmas socks cling and ring. All other gifts they'd unwrapped the day before the move had been stuffed into a box in that lost moving truck.

"You mean it? You're not angry?"

"With you? Nah." The beaming grin Lindsey wore was real. She was proud of Bridget. So proud that it was almost enough to drown out the stab of hurt she had every time she thought of leaving Nebraska and her ballet. Almost. But Bridget was right—

9

the move was her fault. Everything was her fault.

When Mom and Dad told her that Bridget was going to apply for Julliard, she'd thought they were joking. Bridget was only eight! But it turned out that eight was old enough for the pre-college program. Bridget should have started that Fall, but with Grandma's bad health, Dad's work, and other things, they'd had to wait until now. Part of Lindsey hoped Julliard would have changed their mind in that time. But they didn't.

Now, Dad had to work two jobs, and Mom needed to work full time at a café several blocks away. Sure, Bridget had scholarships and grants, but that didn't cover everything. New York was expensive, or that's what Mom and Dad said. Everything they did and every cent they earned went to Bridget.

Lindsey poked at the figurine's tutu, wishing she could squish it, but it bounced right back.

"Mom said your new ballet teacher is really good."

Lindsey kicked her legs out in front of her. They felt stiff. "Yep, that's what Mom said." That didn't mean Mom knew what she was talking about. Classes at the Community Center didn't count as real ballet no matter how well-known the teacher had been. Community Center meant trash. Even if the instructor had been a famous Russian dancer a hundred years ago, no one ever went from Community Center to the New York City Ballet.

Never.

"Bridget? I don't hear you practicing." Mom called again, more tired than angry.

"Yes, Mom." Bridget stuck out her tongue, not that Mom could see, but it made Lindsey smile. A bit.

Before the first notes filled the room, Lindsey flipped onto her side away from Bridget and stared at her music box. The tiny wooden ballerina turned on the pedestal. She'd always spin and be the star of her own little stage. If only Lindsey would have that chance too.

*H*ours later, a moving tower of sleeping bags and pillows blocked the doorway. Underneath, poking out like a pair of chopsticks, were Mom's legs.

"It's going to be another hour or so before we can have lunch," she mumbled from behind the stack as if it had swallowed her alive.

"Really?" Lindsey's stomach rumbled.

"One hour. I promise." Mom backed away with a wobble and turned down the hall.

One hour. Although Lindsey hadn't been hungry before, eating cooked spinach sounded like a treat right now. Or maybe not. A pizza wouldn't have been bad, though.

"Are you hungry, too?"

Bridget nodded. "Yeah. I want pizza."

"That's exactly what I thought!" Lindsey sprang to her feet and charged into the hallway. "Mom?"

The mound of blankets stopped outside of Mom and Dad's bedroom door with a huff and another wobble. "Can't it wait a second?"

Her stomach's rumble made that a definite no. "I could run and get a couple of pizzas. Then, you wouldn't have to worry about anything. There was a sign for a grocery store around the corner. It's really close."

The pile of blankets sank. "I don't know. Are you sure it isn't too far for you to go by yourself?"

"It's not far." Back in Nebraska, Lindsey went everywhere by herself. Even Bridget had been allowed to walk the two blocks to her friend's house alone, and Bridget was four years younger.

A long, heavy breath made the pile fatter than before. "I

know you're accustomed to more freedom, but New York isn't Nebraska. It's more dangerous here. Why do you think we have three locks on the door?"

Lindsey glanced back at the door, sure Mom was joking. Nope. Three dead bolts rowed the edge of the frame, with a chain at the top. As if the locks knew she watched them, they began to turn and clunk—one after the other. Lindsey stepped back, not sure what to expect. Something dangerous, after what Mom had said.

"Honey, I'm home!"

She dove at Dad before he even made it through the door. His fat parka swallowed her face as she squeezed into his waist and breathed in the smell of motor oil and peppermints.

"Whoa! You'd think I hadn't seen you in years."

"Hey, Dad. I bet you're hungry, so starved you could eat a bear." She stepped back to watch him unzip his coat. His head nearly hit the top of the door frame, and his hair poked out in all directions. Melted snowflakes glistened on the ends. His puffy cheeks shone as bright and red as his rounded nose.

"Why? Was one delivered to our door?" he asked.

Mom hurried over and gave him a peck on the cheek. "Lindsey wants to run to the store and pick up some pizzas."

"Sounds good to me. I'll take sausage."

"But do you think that's safe? We just moved here." Mom's forehead wrinkled.

Lindsey knew she worried—a mom thing—but now that she was only three months away from becoming a teenager, Lindsey hoped she'd get over that.

"I thought that's why we moved to this part of Washington Heights. Family friendly. I'm sure she'll be fine." Dad added a wink, the one that always made Mom give in.

"I guess you're right. But I have something she has to have first." Mom headed back down the hall and disappeared into the door on the left.

Lindsey wondered what she was about to get. A cellphone? That'd be neat. Mom and Dad had never allowed her to have one in Nebraska. Maybe New York was different.

12

Dad leaned closer to Lindsey's ear. "She grew up in Nebraska. The big city scares her, but she's not wrong. It is more dangerous here. You'll have to keep your eyes open, even with the thing she's about to give you."

"What is it?"

His answer was a smile. He barely had time to pull back before Mom returned with a black, egg-shaped keychain. She held it between calloused fingers. "Here, take this with you."

Lindsey stared at it. It had one button in the center, and that was it. Not a cellphone. "What is it?"

"An alarm. You push the button, and everyone within a block will hear it. It has 135 decibels." She dropped it into Lindsey's hand. "That's about as loud as an airplane taking off."

Dad peered over her shoulder. "You might want to plug your ears when you use it."

"So, this alarm is great because if no one comes to help me, at least the bad guy will be deaf?"

Mom blinked with confusion. "No. It will scare them away."

Lindsey sighed. Mom must have been overly exhausted to not get the joke.

Dad wrapped an arm around Mom's shoulders. "She's joking, honey."

Never ready to miss a family hug or a hint, Lindsey quickly joined in. "It's great, Mom. Thanks." And it was. Even though the alarm wasn't a cellphone, it got her outside. That was already worth a lot.

With the alarm and money for the pizzas stuffed into her pocket, Lindsey headed out the door. Before going down the stairs, she leaned over the railing and peered down to make sure Witch 2A wasn't still sitting there. Her witch's brew must have been keeping her busy because not a single sound came from the apartment, and the door stayed closed.

"Here it goes." Taking a deep breath, Lindsey dashed down the stairs and out the door.

Rumbling traffic vibrated from the neighboring streets behind a wall of parked cars. The sidewalk in front of the apartment building stretched all the way to the street and was wide enough to play four-square. That was better than nothing. A row of trees growing along the edge towered big and tall, but the lower limbs were chopped away, keeping the branches too high to reach. Lindsey tugged her hood tighter over her head, went down the block, and continued around the corner.

New York was how she pictured it. More or less. Lights, cars, and buildings pushed from every direction. Some stood stubby, some tall and lean, and some stretched out flat as if the next story had been chopped off. People swarmed in both directions, zigzagging as they went. They were bundled tight without smiles or passing hellos. Lindsey kept her head down, only glancing up to make sure she didn't run into anyone or miss the store, which had to be coming up soon.

A high-pitched yip came from the side, and she looked over. Talk about cute! A small terrier tied to a post waggled his tail and barked at the people passing by. No one paid any attention to him, although his super sweetness begged to be petted. Two black circles ran around each eye, giving him the look of a canine nerd, and a tuft of gray fur flopped over his eyes. When a few more people slid by him without the least bit of interest, he whined. *Poor thing.* He was too small to be out in such a big crowd.

"Hi, there." She crouched down and scratched between his ears. "You look like a furry little Einstein. Are you waiting for someone?"

Certain that his owner was inside the store, she gazed through the glass pane. Instead of shelves loaded with things to buy, a large, open room waited on the other side. She rubbed her glove over the glass to clear away the fog and leaned in for a closer look. Colorful figures moved everywhere, swirling, jumping, and flying. *Dancers.*

"Excuse me, darling. I'm afraid my dog isn't as friendly as he appears." A tall, slender woman stepped up from behind, unhooked the dog's leash, and lifted him into her arms.

"Oh, sorry." Lindsey said without looking up. A boy in a purple cape darted past in a row of amazing turns. Behind him, two girls in pink *reveled en pointe*, and then they stretched their legs out behind them into a pair of perfect *arabesques.*

14

"They are spellbinding, aren't they?" the woman asked.

Lindsey nodded, not wanting to look away. Not for a second.

"I'm Madame Destinée. I own this dance school."

When a slender hand appeared next to Lindsey's face, she turned and stumbled to her feet. The second she saw the woman, the statement about owning the dance school hit full force. The dark blue leotard perfectly matched her skirt and tights. Her black hair parted down the middle of her scalp and was pulled so tight into a bun on the back of her head that it must have hurt. She gazed down, batting long eyelashes over a pair of bright red lips. "Do you dance, darling?"

Lindsey started to nod but then stuck out her hand to return the shake. The woman's fingers were boney and icy-cold, but that was no wonder considering it was freezing outside. "I've been taking ballet lessons since I was six."

"Oh my. You must be good. Perhaps you'd like to take lessons here. I bet you'd fit right in." She waved her arm toward the window and the dancers inside.

Lindsey peered back. The studio was amazing, so much better than the one she'd attended in Nebraska. And the dancers were fantastic! Each movement flowed as if they'd been practicing for years.

A girl in red spun by the window. Her skirt swung out like a budding rose. So beautiful! Even if Lindsey was allowed to take classes here—and she already could hear Mom's flat "no"—the dance school owner was wrong. She'd never fit in. She was talented. Sure. But these dancers were genius. It'd take years before she caught up to them.

"Your school looks great, but I'm already signed up for classes somewhere else." It was a good excuse. Too bad it was also true.

"Might I inquire where?"

Lindsey dug her fingernails into the inside of her gloves. "The Community Center," she mumbled.

"Ah, Mr. Lagunov! He's a fine teacher."

Lindsey blinked. Wow. The woman knew him. But he had been famous once, so it probably wasn't super surprising.

15

"My mom said he danced for the Russian ballet," she said.

"That's true. He was extremely talented. How lovely that he's giving classes to the community now. A shame, too."

"Why?"

"His lessons are...umm...let's say lacking. The Community Center simply doesn't have the funding needed to nurture true talent. My school is the finest in the city. I'd say the best in the world, but that would be a bit presumptuous, and we don't want to appear arrogant, do we, darling? You should know that I only accept the best."

On the other side of the window, the girl in red leaped through the air like a shooting comet. So high...she practically flew!

Lindsey's heart sank. She definitely couldn't dance as well as that girl. Even if she wanted to go to this school, once Madame Destinée saw her dance, she wouldn't accept her anyway.

"You mustn't worry about the cost. I'm not interested in money. I only desire your talent."

"You think I'm talented enough to come here?" Lindsey had to have misunderstood. Madame Destinée hadn't seen her dance a single step.

"Yes, darling, I know you are. Your posture speaks for itself. Why don't you come in for a quick trial lesson?"

An icy gust of wind caught Lindsey's scarf, whipping it across her face. As she tucked it back into place, the change in her pocket tinged against the keychain alarm.

"I can't. I have to get going. My mom's waiting for me."

Madame Destinée swished her hand through the air, cutting her off. "It'll take a few moments. Tell your mother you had to wait to get past the garbage truck." She pointed down the street, and sure enough, a garbage truck backed over the sidewalk into the alleyway. The pedestrians swore and went around it, stepping on the street between the cars. Mom would die if she saw Lindsey do that!

When Lindsey looked back, Madame Destinée held a small, red apple in front of the dog's snout. If it had been a dog treat, Lindsey wouldn't have thought much about it, but as far as she knew, dogs weren't apple fans.

16

The dog leaned forward and bit into it with a vicious crunch. As he chewed, drops of juice dripped from his whiskers.

Huh. If she'd known dogs liked apples that much, she would have tried to feed them to one of the neighbor's dogs back in Nebraska. It barked whenever anyone went by its owner's fence.

"You must come inside and take a quick peek. That's all I ask."

Lindsey stared at the truck still parked over the sidewalk. The driver opened his door and climbed out, stretching his legs and yawning as he reached the concrete. He wasn't going anywhere for a while.

"Okay." But only for a few seconds. Hopefully, Mom wouldn't get upset.

The brick hallway inside the school was another mud-colored, worm paradise. It smelled like lemon cleaner and moth balls, too. A few pictures hung along the walls, each showing Madame Destinée in a different ballet pose. Lindsey searched for some photos of the students—every ballet school had them—but there were none.

On the right side, a life-sized photograph caught Lindsey's eye, as if she could miss it if she tried. Madame Destinée wore a beautiful, blue dance dress that shimmered with thousands of tiny crystals like a star-filled sky. It'd been taken while she hung mid-flight in a *grand jeté*, the most elegant one Lindsey had ever seen.

"Lovely, isn't it?" Madame Destinée sighed as she moved in from behind, bringing a breeze with her. "It's been a long time since I've danced like that. Too long."

Her sad whisper made Lindsey wrap her arms around herself and sink into the warmth of her coat. "You were amazing."

"Yes, I *was* amazing. It was long ago." She laid her hand on Lindsey's shoulder and steered her to a door on the left.

She saw no other doors on the left, which was odd considering the hallway stretched on so long.

When Madame Destinée opened the door, a delicious scent rushed out—warm honey, cotton candy, peppermint sticks, and vanilla ice cream all rolled into one. It wasn't anything like the smells found in Lindsey's old dance school, which reeked of

17

sweaty socks.

Expecting to see a table full of food, she peered around Madame Destinée. Instead, bright lights filled the dance studio. Mirrors covered the walls, and the wooden floor glimmered from a fresh polish. In the middle, the dancers swirled.

It was perfect.

Madame Destinée moved to the side of the room and stood there, watching the dancers. She didn't say anything or throw any of them a telling glance. She simply stood there. Back in Nebraska, Lindsey's ballet teacher constantly marched around, telling them to straighten their backs or repeat the steps. Here, everyone danced in their own style and to different beats. It should have been pure chaos, but it fit together better than a carefully planned choreography.

The squeak and soft thumps of the dancers' feet against the floor gave the movement rhythm and beat.

"They practice without music?"

Madame Destinée put one finger to her lips, signaling her to be quiet as the guy in purple spun past. Taking one small leap after another, his feet clunked against the floor.

"They wear earbuds. It helps them to concentrate," she whispered. "Each one dances in a way which allows their talent to bloom. Here, this one should be perfect for you."

She dropped a skin colored plastic thing about the size of a button into Lindsey's hand. One side was flat. The other side had a soft, squishy bump, like bread dough but softer. No matter how often she poked at it, the earbud held its form. How Madame Destinée could know which music would be perfect for her was beyond Lindsey, but it didn't hurt to give it a try.

"Go on. Put it in."

At first, a weird gurgling buzzed in her ear like a distant flushing toilet. Then, there was a beep and a pop, and the music flowed, not the classical pieces that usually played in a ballet class but something with a heavier, faster beat. Madame Destinée gazed over at her and nodded for her to join the others.

Lindsey didn't have to be told twice. She hurried out to the middle of the floor, while the other dancers flew past. Being right in the middle of them was like being caught in a flock of exotic birds. The girls wore sparkling costumes, and some of the guys had on capes—*debonair*. Lindsey's snow boots, thick winter coat, scarf, and hat made her a clumsy, overly rounded snowball.

Darting back to Madame Destinée, she struggled to pull off her scarf.

"Is there a problem, darling?"

"Nope." She tossed the scarf to the side and jerked off her boots, letting them plop to the floor with a pair of thuds. Then, she went back out to the floor. One minute. That's all she needed. She'd dance, and Mom would never know.

Letting the music take over, her feet moved as light as fluttering butterfly wings. *Allegro.* On the far end of the studio, she balanced up on one leg to extend into an *arabesque.* Except her jeans refused to stretch. Fighting back frustration, she went from 2nd position into 5th and *révèle* for what would hopefully be a *pirouette.* As she swung around, the girl in red soared right at her. Lindsey stumbled backward to avoid a collision and plopped down onto her backside with a loud thump.

The whole floor vibrated. Everyone stopped and stared. Lindsey glanced over at her boots and scarf, wanting to crawl under them, hide, and pretend she wasn't there.

Madame Destinée cleared her throat. "Darling, I'm afraid this won't do."

Heat burned Lindsey's face as she pulled herself up from the floor. *Ugh.* It wasn't even her fault. But by the looks on everyone's faces, nobody cared. She should have never agreed to come inside. She did not belong there.

"Come back tomorrow, and we'll try again." With a flick of the wrist, Madame Destinée shooed the dancers back into motion. But the girl in red stood there a second longer with her lips curled into a vicious grin.

Lindsey gathered her stuff and headed toward the door. No way would she come back, even if it were the last dance school on Earth.

$\mathcal{L}$indsey stretched out across her sleeping bag. Bright rays from the morning sun beamed through the window, warming her skin. The heat felt good, but it was the only thing that did. The rest of her ached from sleeping on a dumb, hard floor. One by one, she lifted her arms and legs into the air and dropped them again with a thump. She hoped the moving truck would arrive soon with her fluffy bed or she'd be too stiff to ever move again. After rubbing the sleep out of her eyes, she blinked up at the lonely light bulb dangling from the ceiling. The apartment would never be her home.

"Lindsey, did you take my gloves?" A bloated, green snowsuit appeared in the doorway, topped with a white striped hat and pigtails dangling out on either side. Bridget was so bundled up, it was a wonder she could move. Mom would probably need to roll her to school by the looks of it. "Did you take my gloves? I need them."

Lindsey yawned and stretched her fingers high above her head. "Nope. Haven't seen them."

"Mom! Lindsey stole my gloves and won't tell me where they are!"

Lindsey sat up. "I did not. I haven't seen them." She didn't want to deal with this, not this early in the morning. Scrambling across the floor, she pushed the door shut.

"Mom! Lindsey slammed the door in my face!"

"That's not true! I closed it." Talk about a Miss Cranky Pants!

"Girls, we don't have time for this. Did anyone see my keys?" Mom's rubber-soled shoes clunked past the door.

"Did you look on top of the fridge?" Lindsey called.

The bedroom door creaked open. Mom came in while

zipping her coat over a yellow uniform. A rectangular name tag was pinned to her chest. It read Susan, although her real name was Joan. She didn't want the customers to know her name, especially not here in New York. Dad was right. New York did make Mom nervous.

"Bridget and I have to go now. One of her teachers offered to help her catch up on a few things during Christmas break, so she won't have any problems diving right into the new semester. Your father should be back from the newspaper stand soon. Do you think you'll be all right until he gets home?"

"I guess." Lindsey crawled back to the sleeping bag and jabbed her legs into the warmth.

"I know there's not much for you to do, but you can go down to Ms. Mulberry. She was thrilled when I asked her to help keep an eye on you. She'd like to get to know you. I think she's lonely. Poor woman."

"Who's Ms. Mulberry?" They hadn't met anyone yet, and Mom hadn't mentioned the name before. The one person it could be was... "You mean the lady downstairs?"

"That's her."

Lindsey slid deeper into the sleeping bag until only her head stuck out. Carrying an alarm whenever she walked outside by herself wasn't a big deal, but being stuck with a babysitter was over kill. "I'm too old for a babysitter. Didn't you say Dad's coming home soon?"

"She won't come up here if you don't need her to. And she's very nice. She's the one who suggested your new ballet teacher, Mr. Lagunov."

Lindsey fought not to roll her eyes. "Great." Meaning not great at all, but telling by Mom's slight smile, she didn't get that.

"Go downstairs and visit her. She has a huge collection of classical music. I'm sure you'd know several of the songs from your ballet classes."

"Okay." No way was Lindsey going to go down there.

"Oh, and don't forget your ballet lessons at ten. You know your dad's memory sometimes." She glanced at her watch and tugged the pink hat over her head. "Bridget and I have to get

21

going. Let Ms. Mulberry know if you need anything."

With a sad smile, Mom came over and kissed Lindsey on the head. Her lips felt warm, and although Lindsey wanted to be grumpy, she couldn't help but smile up at her. "Good luck at work."

Mom nodded a last goodbye. Three clunks from the dead bolts later and they were gone.

The ache in Lindsey's legs had left, but now they tingled as if ants had gotten into the sleeping bag. No longer able to sit still, she got up and dressed. If this apartment was her new home, she might as well take a good look at it.

Mom and Dad's bedroom was smaller, but the windows took up an entire wall. When Lindsey gazed out, bricks from the side of the next building stared back at her. The living room was the largest room. The windows let in so much sunlight that it warmed the wooden floor under Lindsey's socked feet. The most interesting room was the bathroom. A huge bathtub loomed in the corner—tons of room for bubbles. A small cabinet stood under the sink with rose-shaped handles. Lindsey crouched down to open the doors, and someone touched her shoulder.

"AHHH!" She jumped, banging her head against the sink.

"Oh, sorry. Are you all right?" Dad's cheeks and nose beamed bright red from the cold.

A dull pain throbbed on the back of Lindsey's head, but as she rubbed it, the sting quickly died away. "Yeah." She fingered the spot. "No bump. I'm fine."

"Are you ready to go to your ballet class?" He rubbed his fingers through his hair, making it stick up even more. "I know it's early, but I thought you might like to have a cup of hot chocolate at one of those cafés on the way."

She dropped her hand, forgetting all about the pain. "A café?" They didn't have any of those in their town in Nebraska, only a corner in the grocery store, which had a couple of tables so that the older farmers could eat donuts. She liked going there, but it would never be as neat as a real café.

The café was two blocks away. The smell of cinnamon filled the store as thick as cotton stuffing. A woman with a purple and black scarf over her head stood behind a counter buried behind all sorts of mugs and cups. Next to the mugs was a brightly painted, roundish pot with a golden spout on the front. *Samovar,* the woman called it. She said it was Turkish and used to make tea.

"Uh, can I have one of the teas?" Lindsey asked when Dad tried to order her a hot chocolate.

The lines around the woman's lips deepened as her smile widened. "It's bitter."

"That's okay." Trying new things was good, or that's what Mom always said. She glided her finger over the golden painting of a flower. It was so pretty.

A table was shoved against the window, and the walls hung so full of colorful scarves and necklaces that it looked as though it might all tumble down. The tea tasted thick, and Lindsey cringed at the first sip, but a few spoonfuls of honey made it delicious. "Mom will love this place."

"I'm sure she will." Dad smiled, not knowing he sported a thick milk mustache from his latte. "We can come here every week if you'd like to. I know things seem unfair with Bridget and Juilliard, but it won't stay that way. One or two years and all will be back to normal."

"It's okay." The lie sat like rocks, but the truth would only make Dad grumpy. Besides, telling him it was unfair didn't change anything.

By the time they reached the Community Center, a small poke of excitement had Lindsey knotting her fingers inside her pockets. Community Center still ranked as trash—the graffiti-filled walls around the doors proved that—but if the teacher was once as famous as Mom and Madame Destinée claimed, then the class might be all right.

Maybe.

A peek inside the building and her hope died a horrible, tormenting death. Lindsey tried to stay positive, but the off-yellow spots staining the ceiling and blue paint flaking from the cinder block walls smothered her attempts. Dad's shoes scuffed with each step as he headed toward the double doors at the end of the hallway. His steps felt as heavy as her heart. He held one door open, offering a half-smile, but it didn't help.

Behind those doors stretched a plain basketball court and not even a nice one. Like the hallway, everything was old, worn, and in need of repair. A handful of girls around Bridget's age sat sprawled across the middle of the court. They wore baggy sweatpants and T-shirts like hip-hop dancers. Half of them had on ballet slippers. Lindsey stared down at her own sweat pants, T-shift and tennis shoes wishing she didn't look like she belonged in the group. But she did.

"Lindsey, this is Mr. Lagunov," Dad said.

Mr. Lagunov came up to Dad's shoulder, but he was three times as round. Ten times hairier, too. He had a mustache and a bushy beard, and his gray hair hung in knotted waves over his ears. It was hard to picture him as a ballet teacher. He looked more like a shaggy, old bear in tights.

Lindsey curtsied as her teacher back in Nebraska had taught her to do.

"Yes!" Mr. Lagunov clapped his hands. The red blotches on his cheeks grew brighter. "That is how it should be done."

Lindsey nodded, not sure if he meant that she'd curtsied correctly or if he was happy that she'd curtsied at all. She decided to go with a little of both.

Mr. Lagunov and Dad discussed pickup times, something she didn't want to listen to but going over to the other girls would be too awkward. She gazed at the CD player on the floor near her feet. The CDs piled next to it had hand-scribbled covers. Some of it was in what she guessed had to be Russian, but she recognized names like Tchaikovsky and Copland. The stack of cut-out newspaper articles next to the CDs was more interesting, though. They were yellowed and written in Russian. One was written in another language, French if she guessed right. She poked at it with her toe until the accompanying photo slid to where she could see it—a ballerina posed with her arms in a beautiful arc over her head.

"Madame Destinée?" She picked it up to get a better look. It sure looked like her but twenty years younger, at least.

"Old men drag too many memories." Mr. Lagunov let out a

24

deep sigh.

"Do you know her?"

He knelt, bringing a wave of soap and something nutty with him. "*Da*, she was a friend many years ago, but then she disappeared. Poof!" He swung his arms through the air in a type of mini-explosion. "Rumors claim she dances in London, Moscow, Paris, and Berlin, all on the same night. That is impossible, but perhaps ghosts are capable of such things."

He thought she was dead. Lindsey gripped the paper tighter, not sure she should say more or not. Her mouth got the better of her. "I saw her. Here in New York." His eyes widened, but her mouth switched into automatic waterfall mode. "I met her yesterday right after we moved in. I was getting pizzas at the store, and I saw her dog. She owns a dance school...a nice one... around the corner from our apartment. I can show you where it is if you'd like."

Mr. Lagunov blinked as if stuck in a brain jam. Then, with a shake of his head, his expression relaxed. "That is a quite the story, but sometimes it's better to let ghosts lie." A tap on the button on the CD player and he turned toward the group of girls waiting on the floor.

Lindsey grumbled. He didn't believe her. He thought she was making up stories like some little kid. The article fluttered from her fingers and landed next to the stack of CDs, but Madame Destinée's eyes gleamed up at her. A happy glisten radiated from them as if she *could* magically dance around the world.

An aching, metallic screech made Lindsey forget the article and swing around. Five girls had followed Mr. Lagunov behind a door on the far end of the gym and were battling to tug out a set of bars for gymnasts. Three sets, scratching so awful it sounded like the entire floor was being scraped off.

"Take your positions," Mr. Lagunov called as the bars were lined up several feet from the wall.

The girls obeyed, giggling and whispering while they held on with one arm and stood straight and tall. Or so they tried. Half of them had banana backs.

"Lindsey, join us."

No mirrors. No real barres.

Following his directions, she ran through every movement and position with the same poise and determination a normal ballet class required. When she closed her eyes and lifted her leg into the air, the world transformed, and she could picture it—a beautiful studio with lights, barres, and mirrors. Taking a deep breath before swinging her leg to the side, she imagined the teacher in Nebraska shouting directions. *Arms straighter. Chins higher.*

"That is good, Lindsey. Very good." Mr. Lagunov's gruff voice cracked her imagination. "Now, we will loosen our joints and muscles."

He waddled over to the CD player, pressed a couple of buttons, and "YMCA" bellowed through the gym. The girls bounced away from the bars, yelping as they ran around in uncontrollable circles.

"That's right. Release the stress and enjoy the freedom of movement."

Lindsey's mouth dropped.

"I know this is probably not what you are used to, but remember, it is Christmas vacation. It is good to have some fun." He winked.

Lindsey forced a smile, but it soured inside like rotten milk. This wasn't a dance class; it was a zoo. And she had to be the biggest monkey ever.

$\mathcal{L}$indsey had never snuck out of the house before. It was stupid. She knew that. Plus, if Mom and Dad were right—and judging by the dead bolts on the apartment door, they might be—New York wasn't exactly the safest place to sneak around alone. Still, Lindsey didn't have a choice. Mr. Lagunov was not a great teacher, no matter what Mom believed. But then again, Mom didn't have a clue about ballet. All she cared about was Bridget. Bridget and her violin.

Lindsey glanced at the dead bolts and took a deep breath.

Dad had left for the warehouse, and Mom wouldn't be back with Bridget until 4:00 pm. That gave her two hours. As for the witch-gone-babysitter...well, she hadn't made a cackle or a peep since Mom left that morning. Lindsey snuggled into her scarf and coat and went to get Mom's extra set of keys from the top of the fridge. Stretching up onto her tiptoes, she nicked the tip of one key. It fell from the fridge and landed on the kitchen counter next to a full bag of apples, right on top of a folded note.

New York—also known as the Big Apple. A present for my busy girls. Dad.

It was sweet, even if she wasn't a huge apple fan. But she knew someone who was. She stuffed an apple into her pocket and left the apartment. Keeping her steps light and quiet, she eased down each stair until she hit the witch's landing. The door stood closed, but a residual cloud of moth balls and lemon cleaner made it clear that the witch lurked nearby.

Lindsey held her breath and listened.

A soft tune, so quiet that the sound of her own heartbeat could've made it impossible to hear, came from behind the door. It sounded like the theme from Swan Lake, but she couldn't be sure. And she didn't care. As long as the witch remained busy, everything was whipped-cream-pie. Keeping her gaze on the door, she slid her feet over the wooden boards—little by little. The second she hit the stairs, she dashed down as fast as she could, all the way outside.

The winter air iced inside her nose as she breathed in. A warm, ketchupy scent soon broke through—hotdogs. On the corner, a small cart with a blue and yellow umbrella blocked half of the sidewalk. The vendor rubbed his hands over the white steam bellowing from below the metal lids. He smiled, but Lindsey kept her head down, not wanting to disappoint him since she still hadn't gotten her allowance that week.

Hotdogs and cool cafés...she needed to ask Mom for a raise. Or Dad. It was always easier to get him to agree.

Ruff. Ruff.

"Whoa!" Lindsey jumped back as a blur of fur pounded into her leg. Madame Destinée's dog pawed her knee once before plopping back down and landing on his haunches. His gigantic doggy grin was impossible to resist.

"Hey, there." She dug the apple out of her pocket and held it out to him. After a careful sniff, he chomped down and tugged it out of her fingers. "Looks like you're hungry." She giggled.

"Ah, so that's why he wanted to come out so badly. You're bribing him." Madame Destinée appeared in the doorway and scooped him up into her arms. "Let's go inside, darling. It's freezing out here, and class is about to begin."

Unlike the last time, she didn't lead Lindsey to the studio but headed toward a door on the right. The only door on the right. Lindsey wondered why she didn't notice it before. But she had been in a hurry. One door on the left, and one on the right. At least, she'd never get lost in this place.

"This is my office." Warmth spilled out as Madame Destinée opened the door and stepped inside.

The room was dimmer than the hallway. Thick, maroon carpet flooded the floor, cushioning Lindsey's every step. A large, oak desk in the middle of the room claimed most of the space. Considering the size of the desk, there wasn't much on it—a picture frame, a bowl of apples, and a pen. One chair stood on either side: a plain, wooden one faced the desk and a big leather one with a high back was behind the desk. The far back wall stretched with plain brick, bare and more boring than the ones in the apartment. A water dispenser claimed one corner. Every now and then, it made a funny *bloop-bloop* sound. The rest of the office stood lined with shelves—bottom to top. They were piled high with music boxes. Hundreds of them.

"I collect them." Madame Destinée motioned to the chair in front of the desk. "They are all handmade originals from the famous toymaker Jeannot Broussard."

Lindsey blinked several times at the huge collection. Every shape. Every color. None appeared to be like the other. "I didn't know he made so many."

"You've heard of him?"

"My grandma gave me one of his music boxes for my birthday." As she gazed over the boxes, she noticed a couple that looked similar to hers.

Madame Destinée came around the desk and grabbed a blue music box from the edge of a shelf as she passed. "I'm sorry, darling, but I'm afraid you're mistaken. The box you own is a copy, not an original. The large toy manufacturers are concerned about profit and will say anything to sell their products...something Jeannot greatly despised."

Lindsey bit her tongue to keep still, but words fought to break free. Grandma would have never given her a copy of anything. Never. She was particular about things like that.

"My brother and I were close. That's why I've kept every single one of his music boxes, all three-hundred and nineteen. I couldn't dare part with a single one."

Lindsey blinked as Madame Destinée's words hit. "Wait. Jeannot Broussard was your brother?"

"Is. I'm holding onto hope. He disappeared, but I'm certain he'll return one day." She laid the music box onto Lindsey's lap. "These boxes remind me not to give up hope."

Lindsey rubbed her finger over the blue flower petals in the center of the lid. Jeannot Broussard had been Madame Destinée's brother. That meant he had disappeared during *her* performance. How terrible that must have been! If the same thing had happened to her and Bridget had disappeared, Lindsey was sure she'd never stop crying again. She peered up at Madame Destinée and wondered how the teacher could talk about her brother so calmly. It was clear she missed him.

It made the music box in her hand so much more precious.

"There's no reason for you to look so glum." Madame Destinée leaned back against the desk. "I'm not lonely. I have Broussard to keep me company."

With a bark, the dog circled Madame Destinée's feet once before flopping down onto his back. She knelt and scratched his belly. "Now, darling, I want you to flip the music box over and rub your finger across the lower edge, directly below the area between the metal hinges."

Scared she might accidentally drop the box and break it, Lindsey gripped the sides with her hands and turned it over. Placing her finger on the spot as Madame Destinée had suggested, she rubbed the edge of the box. Golden letters appeared—a signature with swirly swoops and curls. After a second or two, it faded away again.

"Wow. I never noticed that on my music box."

"Of course not. The original boxes carry the mark." She held out her hand.

Before returning it, Lindsey rubbed her finger across the spot again and watched the signature appear and fade. "Neat," she whispered and handed it back to Madame Destinée.

"Let's get back to you, darling. Despite your unfortunate display yesterday..." She let the words fade as she studied Lindsey from head to toe.

Lindsey didn't need to see her tightening lips and lowering eyebrows to know the sweatpants and T-shirt she wore at the moment weren't acceptable attire either.

"Please, darling, tell me you at least brought your ballet slippers."

Lindsey squished further back against the chair and shook

her head. She knew what was coming next—Madame Destinée would send her home. It was a mistake to come back there.

"I'm certain you have an explanation. Am I correct?" Madame Destinée gazed at her, waiting.

"I'm sorry. It's just that our clothes haven't gotten here yet. Everything's still in a box in the moving van. My mom made me take my dance clothes out of the suitcase to fit in the music box. She was afraid it might break otherwise."

"The copy of my brother's?"

Lindsey nodded.

"Well then, I can't blame her or you for that." She pulled away from the desk, and with a swirl, went to the office door. "Come, darling. It's time for you to show me how you truly dance, even if it is in socked feet."

The dance studio appeared exactly the same as the day before: yummy smells, colorful lights, and dancers with beautiful costumes. Except this time, nausea twisted and churned at Lindsey's stomach the minute she stepped inside.

Madame Destinée pushed the earbud into her hand. "You may warm-up on the barres first."

The barre—a real one—felt warm and smooth under Lindsey's fingers. After stretching up and down on her toes a couple times and doing a few basic *pliés*, she placed her feet in 5th position. Making sure to hold her back and head as straight as possible, she did a *grand plié*.

"Try a *grand battement*, darling."

She slid her feet into 3rd position and threw her leg through the air. The girl in red hurried to the barre and performed a *grand battement,* too. Then, the girl turned to her out-stretched leg, bent over, and placed her forehead against her knee.

It was perfect.

Lindsey's fingers slid off the barre as she dropped her leg. She couldn't do that. Not even close. Madame Destinée was wrong. She didn't belong here. She wasn't as good as the rest of the dancers.

Madame Destinée waved her hand and motioned her to join the others already dancing around the studio. Lindsey obeyed even though it was a waste of time. It'd take months...no, years... for her to catch up to everyone else there. *At least, there was still Mr. Lagunov.* The thought didn't help.

As soon as Lindsey came to the center of the floor, the music played, and she let it take her away. The tempo hit with a race, and she went with it. In tiny steps, she *bourréed* across the studio. Faster and faster she went until she swirled into a whirlwind spin. When the last note fell away, her entire body vibrated as if she'd just gotten off a loopty-loop roller coaster ride.

It was amazing! Every part of her felt as if it might explode. This was what dancing was about. Nothing else made her feel so alive and free.

As she sucked in breath after breath, she realized no other dancers moved around her. Sweat dripped down the side of her face as she slowly turned, hoping she hadn't missed something. But she must have because the other dancers were gone. The studio lay empty.

"That was lovely!" Madame Destinée waited on the side, with a grin on her face. "I'm never wrong. You are indeed talented."

Lindsey automatically curtseyed. With the earlier doubt swept away, her face pulled into a humongous grin. She'd done it! Never had dancing felt so easy. Sure, she was tired, but she didn't even need to stop and take a break. She could have danced for hours.

Madame Destinée came forward and squeezed her shoulders. "You must be absolutely famished after that. All of my dancers are after working so hard. That's why I make sure there's enough food for everyone when the practices are done."

She motioned to the side. A long table stood by the wall, piled high with every food imaginable: oranges, hamburgers, French fries, and all sorts of other dishes Lindsey didn't recognize. But they looked great. Amazing. She wanted to eat them all.

Her mouth watered as she grabbed a plate and stared down the row. Near the end lay a platter of exotic fruits, even star shaped ones. Next to it was a plate of pink donuts with colored sprinkles. Bridget loved those. If she'd been there, she would have eaten half a dozen. Lindsey snatched a nearby napkin, wrapped up a doughnut and stuffed it into her pocket.

"There's no reason to be shy. I know donuts and cakes seem a bit out of line, but my younger students do love them. I use a special recipe to insure they're as healthy as a piece of fruit."

Lindsey spotted a platter piled high with white, fluffy cream puffs. Without thinking, she jabbed her finger into one, pulled out a giant mound of cream, and jammed it into her mouth. Thousands of tiny, sugary giggles popped free and bounced around inside her.

"This tastes great," she mumbled, with her mouth full of cream. It was hard to believe they were healthy, but there was no reason to doubt Madame Destinée. A dance teacher would never lie about something important like that; only healthy dancers were top dancers.

"It's a secret ingredient I picked up from a dear friend years ago. Go ahead. Take as many as you like. You'll need your strength for tonight's show."

The last bite choked. "There's a show tonight?"

"Yes, darling. All of my dancers perform in the nightly shows, every night. That's the payment for the lessons. But don't fret. It's in a gorgeous theatre with a fabulous stage. And it's always sold out."

"The shows are every night?" Uncertainty laced with panic made her choke on the last bite, but when she swallowed the cream, doubt disappeared in a wave of wonderful sensations. Happiness tickled down her throat, through her stomach, and all the way to her toes.

"Yes, every night."

Lindsey stared at Madame Destinée, ready to say that there was no way she could dance in nightly shows. But the giggles inside wanted her to agree right away. This was her chance. She'd always dreamed of dancing on a real stage. She couldn't say no.

But there was one problem—Mom and Dad would never approve.

Madame Destinée cleared her throat. "I expect you to be here at quarter to midnight and not a second later."

"I don't know..." She could sneak out, she guessed. Mom

33

and Dad probably wouldn't notice. But it was one thing to sneak out of the apartment during the day and another to do it in the middle of the night. In the dark. Alone. On the streets of New York. For a moment, she understood Mom's fear. A shiver raced through her, but the tingly excitement swung back in to fight it. It was like a tug-a-war, and she was the rope in between.

"If you don't agree, I'm afraid I can't give you lessons. Those are my rules."

Lindsey set her plate on the table and stared at it. She'd never enjoyed dancing as much as she had a few minutes ago, and that was saying a lot considering she loved dancing more than anything else. The thought of giving that up and staying with Mr. Lagunov...well, it stunk.

"I understand if you can't agree. And it's not as if you'd give up dancing entirely. You'd still have the classes at the Community Center."

The sound of the screeching gymnastic bars echoed in Lindsey's ears.

"What a shame it will be not to have you dance on that stage. I am certain the audience would have loved you, considering how talented you are. You would have become the star."

Lindsey let out a long, aching breath. *A star.* Even if she was the best dancer in the world, nobody would ever notice her at the Community Center. It was a dead end. The closest she'd get to a real stage during her life would be watching Bridget from the audience. She wanted to watch Bridget play her violin, but that wasn't enough. She wanted to be on the stage dancing and making the audience cheer. That was her dream, one that would never come true if she turned down Madame Destinée.

"The shows are only an hour, darling. No one would notice you'd gone. You will dance, and the audience will cheer for you every night. Even your parents will be proud when you become famous. And you will, darling. You will become famous."

Lindsey closed her eyes. Mom and Dad would be proud, but not if they caught her sneaking out before she could reach stardom. She'd be grounded for eternity and stuck with that witchy neighbor as a babysitter for the rest of her life.

"I have something that might help." Madame Destinée bounded off across the studio in a row of perfect *pirouettes*. On the other side, she bent down and took something from a short cabinet. When she returned, she held a small metal box in her hand. "Use this and no one will notice you left."

Lindsey peered at the silver cube. "What is it?"

"A music box. A special music box." She placed the box in Lindsey's hand.

Lindsey turned the cube over and over. There wasn't anything special about it. It was just a plain metal box.

"Place this in your parents' bedroom before you leave tonight. Tap the top of it three times, and a melody will soothe them into a deep sleep. It's harmless hypnotism. When you return, tap it three times, and the song will end. It's like magic. But what music isn't magical?"

If what Madame Destinée said was true—and Lindsey had no reason to doubt her—the box would make it easy for her to sneak out.

"Your parents will never know," Madame Destinée whispered as if reading Lindsey's thoughts. "Plus, you want to become a star, no?"

Lindsey stared down at her socked feet. If Mom cared even a tiny bit about her ballet, then she would have let her at least pack the ballet slippers. They didn't take up much space. But mom didn't care. Madame Destinée was right. If Lindsey wanted to dance on a real stage, she'd have to take the risk. She stuffed the box into her pocket and nodded.

Yes, she was ready to do what had to be done. She would become a star.

$\mathscr{L}$indsey lay in her sleeping bag that night with her eyes closed, but there was no way she could fall asleep. Her stomach wiggled and wobbled more than a bowl full of worms at the idea of sneaking out in a few minutes. To make things worse, every time she started to drift off, car brakes squealed, a door banged, or someone yelled outside. Nobody could sleep with all that noise. New York was not a quiet place.

Rolling over onto her side, she picked up her music box from the floor. Madame Destinée insisted that it wasn't an original made by Jeannot Broussard, that it was a fake. Turning it upside down, Lindsey brought it into the beam of moonlight shining through the window and rubbed her thumb over the spot she had been shown earlier. Sure enough, the golden signature glistened clear—Jeannot Broussard with a funny swirl at the end.

"I knew it." She slapped her hand over her mouth. She hadn't meant to say it out loud!

Bridget let out a moan, kicked her leg up, held it in the air for a second, and then let it flop to the floor with a thud. Then came the snore. If snoring was a musical talent, Bridget would have gained acceptance to Julliard soon after she was born.

Setting the music box back on the floor, Lindsey gazed over at the digital alarm clock near Bridget. 11:24 pm.

Time to go.

She'd been lucky—Mom had been too tired to check if she and Bridget had put on their pajamas before going to bed. Still in sweat pants and a hoodie, Lindsey carefully pulled the special music box from Madame Destinée out from her pocket and tiptoed past Bridget into the hallway.

Getting out of the bedroom without waking up Bridget was

easy. Entering Mom and Dad's bedroom was a whole different story. Dad wasn't the problem. His snore rattled the walls worse than Bridget's. It was whisper-and-she's-awake Mom—as Dad called her—who Lindsey had to watch out for.

Lindsey's fuzzy socks slid over the floor, cushioning each step. A ninja couldn't have been sneakier. Mom grunted. Lindsey froze and waited. Mom pulled the blankets tighter over her head. Soon, steady breathing returned. Lindsey continued into the room and set the music box cube on the floor directly behind the door frame. She tapped it three times. A light melody chimed, a lullaby barely louder than a whisper. In a few seconds, Dad's snoring faded into gentle breathing.

"Mom? Dad?" she whispered.

They didn't stir.

"Mom? Dad?" She used her normal voice and cringed, ready for Mom's questions.

But none came. Mom slept and slept and slept.

"Wow." It was neat and gave her goose bumps at the same time. She'd heard of hypnotism and seen it on TV but witnessing it in real life was strange. That a simple song could knock people out cold was scary, too. If burglars used such a device, they'd never get caught.

Using the music box on Mom and Dad felt wrong too. Lindsey stared at the metal rectangle. Part of her wanted to forget the whole thing, but if she did that, she'd be back to where she was before—nowhere. This was her only chance. If she didn't take it, she'd be left sitting in the audience while Bridget performed on stages across the country or even the world.

She couldn't let that happen.

Shoving guilt away, Lindsey tiptoed across the living room to the kitchen, snagged the spare keys off the fridge, and unlocked the dead bolts with a gentle *clunk-clunk-clunk*. She went down the stairs, careful to make sure they didn't creak. At the witch's door, she stopped. It was closed. She leaned closer and listened. The only sound came from her heart beating in her chest. But she'd better not take any chances. Imaging each step to be as light as a feather, she continued down the stairs.

Outside, the sidewalk glimmered white. Snow billowed up in gusts as the wind groaned a ghostly tune. A shiver ran down her spine as she reached to zip up her coat.

Her fingers hit pure sweatshirt.

"Ugh." With all of her sneaking, she'd forgotten to grab her coat. Snowflakes collected on her eyelashes and tickled her nose. Hugging herself, she hoped it'd keep her warm, but it didn't. It was cold and snowy. Still, there was no way she could go back in and get her coat. Hopefully, she wouldn't freeze before she got to the school.

The warmth inside the school engulfed her like a fuzzy quilt. Lindsey glanced down at her boots and the mini-puddles forming beneath them. The rest of the floor was clean and glistening as if it'd been freshly mopped. Hopefully, she wouldn't get scolded for making a mess. But when she gazed down the hallway, nobody was there anyway.

The light above her head buzzed. She brushed the snow off her hair, wondering where everyone was hiding. Madame Destinée had said quarter to midnight.

"Hello?"

The light flickered.

Trying to stay calm, she grabbed her wet hair, twisted it into a bun on top of her head, and secured it with a hair tie from around her wrist. Taking a deep breath, she went to the office door. Light glowed from beneath it. So, she knocked.

"Ah, Lindsey, come in," Madame Destinée said. "You're right on time. That's wonderful. I have something for you."

Her blue leotard had been replaced with a midnight blue dance dress. The skirt swished and fluttered up around her like delicate flower petals as she strode behind her desk. She leaned down to take something out from a drawer. "Here is your costume, darling. You'll need it for the performance."

Lindsey took the blue bundle—her favorite sky-over-cornfields blue. She rubbed her fingers over the fabric. So soft! And it shimmered with the dust of tiny stars.

"Let me show you to the changing room. You must get ready for the show. The audience eagerly awaits your performance tonight."

Lindsey froze. "Wait. I'll be dancing?"

"Of course." Madame Destinée didn't even flinch a smile.

But it had to be a joke. "How can I dance?" She'd taken one class, and she hadn't learned choreography or anything. There was no way she could perform on a stage. Definitely not in a show.

"You're the most talented dancer I've come across in years. You honestly don't think I'd let you stand in the shadows and watch."

Yes. Yes, she did, and she wanted to tell Madame Destinée that, but the woman was already spinning out of the room.

"Come along. We are in a bit of a hurry, darling."

All sorts of reasons why she couldn't perform zoomed through Lindsey's head as she followed Madame Destinée out into the hallway. If Madame Destinée would have stopped long enough to let her, Lindsey would have told her every single one. But the teacher was caught up in an endless row of spins until she reached another door further down the hallway.

A door on the right.

Lindsey halted. The door hadn't been there before. She was sure of it. There'd been two: one on the left, and one on the right. But there it was, a solid brown wood with a golden handle curved up like a smile.

"There's a door here?"

Madame Destinée cocked an eyebrow. "Every changing room has a door."

Which was true, but still, there was no way Lindsey couldn't have noticed it before. But she must have overseen it somehow because it was right there. She glanced up and down the hallway, making sure the only other doors were to the studio, office, and the entrance—

A bright light burst forth as Madame Destinée opened it. Lindsey coughed against a cloud of perfume and hairspray.

The first glance disappointed. Unlike the studio and office, the changing room was like any other changing room—gray linoleum floor, puke yellow walls, and wooden benches with a row of metal hooks on the wall over them. About a dozen girls scuttled around while they dressed into their costumes. No one looked up as she entered.

"Hurry, darling. You don't want to keep the audience waiting." Madame Destinée flashed a last smile and let the door fall shut as she disappeared back into the hallway.

Finding a free spot in the corner, Lindsey laid the costume down: a leotard, matching tights, and a slick wrap skirt with silver threads along the edges. It shimmered but not as much as the costume on the girl standing across from her—the girl in red from the day before. Her tutu fluffed around her like a budding rose full of glitter. With her long, black hair and dark skin, she reminded Lindsey of a Spanish Flamenco dancer.

"I saw you dancing. You're amazing," Lindsey offered. Normally, she wouldn't have said anything, but she couldn't help it. The girl was good.

The girl wrinkled her nose, tossed her hair over her shoulder, and turned away.

"That was a compliment," Lindsey mumbled.

"Ignore her." A girl about a year or so younger than Lindsey sat on the bench with her knees pulled up under her chin. Her black hair was pulled into a beautiful ball on top of her head with a poof of curls which cascaded over her ears. Her yellow dress dazzled against her dark skin, making her beam like a ray of sunshine, except for the frown on her face.

"That's Adela. She thinks she's special." She pushed her chin down harder against her knees. "I'm Ellie."

"Lindsey."

The girl had a nice accent, which made every word sound like a song. Lindsey wanted to ask about it but wasn't sure if that would be rude or not. Instead, she put on her costume and finished straightening her skirt.

"Pretty." Ellie watched from over her knees.

"Thanks." Lindsey plopped down onto the bench and peered back at Adela. That was a mistake. Adela glared fire.

"Why is she angry with me?"

"You're wearing blue. That's Madame Destinée's favorite

40

color, the color of the dress she wore during her last performance. You saw the picture in the hallway?"

Lindsey shrugged. "Yeah, and?"

"No one wears blue. Adela's scared it means that you're Madame Destinée's new favorite." Ellie rolled her eyes.

"I can't be her favorite. I just got here."

"But still, you have blue."

It was a stupid reason for Adela to be upset, and Lindsey doubted it was true. There had to be more than that, not that she knew what it could be. Lifting one leg up and hugging her knee to her chest, Lindsey tried to make herself as small as possible. She didn't want to stick out. Each of these girls was a much better dancer than her. She'd seen them. They were amazing, especially Adela.

The other girls sat on the benches in groups of twos or threes. Wishing she could fit in, she tried to listen to what some of them were saying, but everyone spoke in a different language. Two girls were dressed in pink and had to be twins. Their hair bobbed off at their chins, and they crossed their legs, left over right, while babbling away in French—she knew that because Mom could speak a little French. Another pair of girls in the opposite corner spoke Russian. At least, they sounded a lot like Mr. Lagunov. Along the other wall, there was a group of girls who must have been from somewhere in Asia, and another that Lindsey guessed must come from Africa. But she couldn't be sure. The words they spoke didn't sound like anything she'd heard before.

Dad said New York was a big melting pot. He was right.

"Where do you come from?" Ellie asked.

Lindsey smiled from behind her leg, glad that at least Ellie was talking to her. "My family just moved here from Nebraska. We have an apartment around the corner."

Ellie shook her head. "No, I mean which city do you live in? I can tell by your accent you're American."

Lindsey scrunched up her nose at the odd question. "Well now, I live here in New York."

"I live in Stockholm. That's in Sweden."

"Sweden?" That was in northern Europe if Lindsey

remembered correctly. She didn't know much about Sweden, only that Dad had a CD from a Swedish music group, which gave her a headache whenever he played it. The cover portrayed a blond woman wearing a wreath of flowers around on her head. He claimed it was a very traditional setting and matched their culture.

Ellie was not blond.

Lindsey must have stared at her a little too long because after a few seconds, Ellie huffed and rolled her eyes. "Yes, I know I don't look Swedish. My parents were from Somalia. That's in Africa. They immigrated to Sweden before I was born. In Stockholm, there are many people who came from countries like Iraq, Afghanistan—"

"Wow. It's more of a melting pot than New York." Lindsey offered an apologetic smile as she realized she'd interrupted Ellie. "Sorry, but that's what my dad calls New York."

Ellie nodded and then looked over to Adela. "She lives in Santiago, Chile. The girl next to her, Tiana, lives in Mexico City. The two in purple come from St. Petersburg, Russia, and the ones in pink live somewhere in France. I'm sure most of them can speak English when they want to."

Gazing at all the girls and hearing the harmony of all the languages made Lindsey feel smaller than before. Madame Destinée said she took the best in the world. If each of these girls were in New York to attend her dance school, they had to be good. Very good. Her tongue rubbed over the top of her mouth, sticky and dry.

"How long have you been here?" Lindsey asked.

Ellie stared at the ceiling, appearing to be in deep thought. "I'm not sure. A couple of weeks? My time is almost done."

"Already?" Two weeks was way too short!

"Madame Destinée only needs two or three weeks to decide if we're good enough to remain and move into her private lessons. If not, we're asked to leave."

Madame Destinée hadn't mentioned that before. Two weeks wasn't enough time for her to learn anything. Maybe that whole star talk had been a lie after all.

She rested her chin on her knee and watched the other girls. Most came from halfway around the world to attend the school. It didn't seem fair to send them home after two weeks if they weren't as good as Madame Destinée had hoped.

"Well, at least I live around the block. The rest of you will have to fly all the way back home if she doesn't accept you."

Ellie shook her head. "No, you don't understand. We don't have to fly anywhere. We are home."

"But I thought you said everyone lives in different places around the world?"

"They do." Ellie gave a heavy sigh as if explaining this grew tiresome. "Everyone lives in their own homes around the world, but we all come to Madame Destinée's dance school in our own cities at the same time for practices and shows."

Lindsey stared at her. Ellie must have been having trouble with her English because what she said didn't make any sense.

"Yeah, I get it." She smiled and nodded because she didn't get it, but that didn't matter. She was impressed with Ellie's English as it was, and she liked talking to her. She seemed like someone who could become a good friend.

Everyone jumped to their feet and fell into a curtsey. Even Ellie.

"What's going on?" Lindsey asked as she did the same.

Before Ellie could answer, Madame Destinée hurried to the center of the room.

"Darlings, it's showtime!"

$\mathcal{M}$adame Destinée clapped her hands twice. The dancers formed a line in front of the door. Lindsey moved to the end behind one of the Asian girls, who wore a costume of red, black, and gold. Smiling, the girl turned and bowed her head before saying something in another language.

Lindsey found it fascinating.

"Sanae Aito," the girl said, pointing to herself.

Lindsey stared at her a moment before it clicked. "Lindsey." She smiled back.

Sanae Aito nodded, and then she turned to face the front of the line. She stuck out her hand, holding it stiff like a waiter with a serving tray. Since all the other dancers did the same, Lindsey followed along. Madame Destinée went down the row, balancing a silver tray full of pink, bite-sized cakes on one hand: petit fours.

"Here you go, little darlings." Using her thumb and forefinger, she carefully placed one in each of their hands, and then she placed an earbud next to it. When she got to Lindsey, she paused. "I know you might not be hungry, darling, but this will do wonders for your nerves." She winked as she placed a petit four on the palm of Lindsey's hand. "And the earbud goes in right before you enter the stage."

A tiny pair of pink candy pointe shoes decorated the center of the square cake. Lindsey bit off a small piece at the corner. Vanilla. She popped the whole thing into her mouth and chewed. The taste exploded with sweet fireworks. Delicious! Happy tingles spread down her throat and into her stomach, so bubbly that she had the urge to burp. Placing her hand over her mouth, she cringed in embarrassment at what was about to happen. But instead of a burp, giggles burst from her lips. Soon, the entire dressing room filled with laughter, and not only hers. Each dancer giggled, the smiles growing on their faces by the second.

With snorts, giggles, and one girl even blasting in a hideous laugh, they filed out into the hallway.

Madame Destinée stood outside the changing room door, not saying a word about the giggle frenzy. But her jaw was clenched. Hard.

Lindsey kept her lips pushed tight together to hold the giggles back as best she could, but they snorted through her nose as she went by Madame Destinée. "Sorry," she whispered, hoping she wouldn't become angrier. The woman scowled fiercely already.

The blue dress fluttered behind Madame Destinée when she hurried back to the front of the line. As Lindsey watched, she realized which flower the dress reminded her of: a dark blue violet. It was one of the few flowers Mom didn't like. She claimed they were a death omen.

The girls marched down the hallway to a staircase at the end, where Madame Destinée stepped aside and allowed them to climb up before her.

Lindsey blinked, not sure what to think. The staircase hadn't been there before, or at least, she hadn't seen it. Not that she knew how she could miss it. The staircase was huge and grand! When she came to Madame Destinée, she hesitated.

"Is something wrong, darling?"

A giggle burst out as soon as Lindsey opened her mouth, but she did her best to ignore it. "Were the stairs here earlier today?" It sounded like a stupid question, even to her own ears, so she backtracked and tried again. "I mean, I didn't notice them before. I thought the hallway ended here." It still sounded dumb, but she couldn't change that. The whole thing was weird, and she was positive the stairs hadn't been there before.

"I had them built a few minutes ago."

Lindsey's mouth dropped. "Wow. Really?"

"Of course not, darling. No one could build stairs as wonderful as these that quickly. They've been here for years. That's why I insisted you eat my cake before going on stage. It calms the nerves." She must have seen the confusion in Lindsey's face because she took a deep breath and stepped closer. "Many things influence how we perceive the world around us. You were nervous the first two times you visited my school, so it's no wonder you weren't able to notice something as unimportant as a staircase at the end of the hallway, especially when the lights weren't on at that time."

That wasn't true. She had looked carefully, and there hadn't been a staircase. "But—"

Madame Destinée raised her hand to stop her. "It is snowing outside, freezing, and has been for the last couple of days. You know that very well. Yet, you were so nervous before coming here you overlooked that fact and forgot your coat. So you see, being nervous can make us blind to usually obvious things." She tilted her head and blinked, daring Lindsey to disagree.

The stairs were obviously there, and Madame Destinée's explanation sounded reasonable. Although Lindsey still couldn't believe she'd overlook something like an entire staircase, she couldn't argue with the facts. At the staircase, she slid her hand over the railing. The dark wood was smooth and warm. Gold laced the edge of each stair and along the banister, too. Trying not to step on the gold trim, she hurried to catch up to the rest of the line.

At the top of the stairs was a backstage room. A dim, orangish-yellow light glowed from a single light bulb above them. On the far end of the room, a red curtain hung from the ceiling and pooled over the floor. A muffled rumble of voices seeped through from behind it. Lindsey had never seen a real backstage area before, but this was exactly the way she'd pictured one to be. Except for the smell. The place stunk as if something had died in the corner and no one had bothered to take it away.

Gagging, she pressed her hand against her nose. If the theatre was as grand as Madame Destinée claimed, it shouldn't stink so badly.

"Here, this will help."

A cool, wet spray hit her neck as she noticed the row of boys lining up beside them.

She jerked her head to the side to find a boy staring at her.

He was about her age but a little taller. He flipped his head to the side, but dark hair still hung over his eyes.

"What did you spray on me?" she demanded, sure he'd played a practical joke.

He held up a small bottle in front of her before turning away and setting it down on a cardboard box along the wall.

"I borrowed the perfume from my grandmother because it stinks up here. I'm Robert." He drew his purple cape over his shoulder and gave a smile. Dimples deepened on his cheeks. They reminded her of a boy in her school back in Nebraska. That kid shot spitballs at her hair. But something told her Robert wouldn't do that. His eyes were sky blue, her favorite color. Jerks couldn't have eyes like that.

"Lindsey," she said.

A cranking noise and the rustle of the curtain drew her attention back to the front of the line.

"Show time," he whispered as he left and followed the rest of the boys onto the stage. "And don't forget the earbud," he called back before disappearing through the curtain.

The earbud slipped between her shaking fingers, and she almost dropped it. The girls in front of her already filed onto the stage, leaving her to shove the earbud into place and catch up to them. At the curtain, she hesitated. This was crazy! She couldn't go out onto a stage, not without knowing how or what to dance! She'd make a fool out of herself. It'd be a million times worse than landing on her backside during practice. This time an entire audience sat and watched. They'd laugh at her. Every single one.

"Come on, darling. It's time."

Madame Destinée grabbed her arm and pulled her forward. Before Lindsey realized what happened, she stumbled toward the other dancers and barely caught her balance to avoid plowing into Saneo Aito.

"Sorry," she whispered.

If Sanae Aito heard her, she didn't show it. Her eyes concentrated on something out in the audience.

Lindsey took her place next to her and peered in the same

direction, but bright lights beamed down from all directions, making it impossible to see anything. Everything beyond the front edge of the stage sat in a black void. Still, the audience was there, waiting. She could feel their anticipation dripping down her neck like icky ooze.

Finally, the music played.

The stage and the audience disappeared. Lindsey spun and danced, gliding across the stage. The music embraced her like a warm hug and invited her to fly.

One *pirouette*.

Two.

She bounded high into the air. A pair of arms caught her, steadying her before swishing away into a joint spin.

The music stopped. Lights beamed down from all directions.

"Ready to come down?" Robert stared up at her. He held her high in the air; her body stretched out above him in a lift.

Lindsey sucked in air. She was going to fall! She had no idea how she got up there. His quivering arms made her wish she hadn't. "If you drop me, I swear I'll pour that whole bottle of perfume over your head. You'll stink like your grandma for weeks."

He laughed, which didn't exactly help things. The muscles in his arms tightened against his sleeves as he lowered her. Her weight shifted one way and then the other. When her feet hit solid floor, she let out a sigh of relief.

"Bravo! Bravo!" The theatre shook.

The audience! Lindsey turned to face the crowd. It was impossible to see them past the bright stage lights, but their cheers made it clear they were there.

"Bravo! Bravo!"

The other dancers lined up on either side of them, all falling into a wave of bows and curtseys. Robert took her hand, and together they stepped forward and accepted the applause.

Ruf. Ruf. Ruf.

"Broussard?" Squinting, Lindsey finally made out the first row of chairs. The red velvet cushions were puffed up and lined with golden cord. And every single one of them was empty. She couldn't see past the first row to the rest of the theatre Not that it mattered. Telling by the cheers, the rest of the seats were full.

"Smile and wave," Robert ordered as he pulled her behind him and followed the rest of the dancers off the stage.

And she did smile and wave, as big and thankful as she could. She didn't know how the music had made her dance, but, at the moment, she didn't care. The audience loved the show, and she loved dancing for them. This was what it was like to dance on a real stage. It was better than she'd dreamed. She belonged on a stage. She was born for it.

"That was amazing!" Ellie pulled off her tights and flung them through the air, almost slapping Lindsey in the nose. "You and Robert were perfect! You are soul mates. That doesn't happen often—two people experiencing the music together. A *pas de deux!*"

Lindsey yanked her shirt over her head. Thanks to her shaky hands, she got it knotted over her bun and had to take the shirt off and try again.

"I'm sure Madame Destinée will take both of you on now. You're so lucky!"

Robert was nice, she supposed, and it was fun to dance with him—the lift had been amazing. But a soul mate? *Ick.* That sounded weird. It was time to change topics. Fast.

"Why was the front row of chairs in the theatre empty?" It was an odd question, but it was the first thing to pop out of her mouth.

"Oh, the chairs? Those are always empty. Madame Destinée doesn't want anyone close to the stage. She claims it is better to leave the distance to the audience. Makes for less…" She pushed her lips together and hummed as if in thought trying to think of the correct word.

"Distractions?" Lindsey offered.

"Yes! That's it. Madame Destinée doesn't want us dancers to be distracted. The rest of the seats were sold out, all three-hundred. Can you believe the theatre has three hundred and twenty-four seats?" Ellie added with a shrug.

Three hundred people had watched them perform. Although Lindsey knew many theatres held a much larger audience than that, it was still amazing. Three hundred people had seen her dance.

A small screech from a girl at the end of the row of benches made everyone freeze and look up. Madame Destinée stood in the doorway with Broussard cradled in her arms. Her lips pushed into a tight line of concentration as she gently glided her fingers over his back. One by one, she gazed over the girls.

The other dancers straightened, gripping their knees so tight their knuckles turned white. Lindsey scooted to the edge of the bench and bit her lower lip. If excitement worked like static electricity, there would have been fireworks. She wished she knew why everyone was so nervous.

Madame Destinée closed her eyes, raised her nose high into the air, and sniffed. With deliberate steps, she sauntered down the row, sniffing the air above each girl. Once or twice, her nose twitched, and the eyes of the girl in front of her grew wide and bright, but then Madame Destinée shook her head and continued.

Lindsey sniffed, trying to figure out what she was looking for. The room smelled sweaty, like dirty socks, and the mixture of fruit and flowers made it clear that Robert wasn't the only one carrying around a bottle of perfume. But that's all her nose found.

When Madame Destinée reached Adela, she jerked to a halt. She sniffed, and her nose twitched. She sniffed again, and her nostrils flared. Adela slid forward to the edge of the bench and cleared her throat.

With a snort, Madame Destinée moved on.

Adela sank into a sad lump.

The sniffing resumed. Each girl slid forward on the bench to get closer to Madame Destinée's amazing nose. Without sniffing Ellie or Lindsey, she stepped out into the middle of the room.

"Sanae Aito, join me in my office."

Sanae Aito stood and gave a bow of her head. Before she left the room, though, her lips twitched into a smile.

"I hope she's chosen for private lessons," Ellie whispered from the side.

Lindsey nodded. So, that's what this was about. Sanae Aito's time was up, not that Lindsey knew what that had to do with all of the sniffing. *Weird.* Either way, she hoped Sanae Aito was chosen to stay for the private lessons, too. Then someday, she may have a chance to talk to her more.

"Lindsey."

Lindsey jerked her head up toward Madame Destinée. "Yes?"

"I'd like to speak with you about another matter. Stay here until I call you to my office."

"But my parents—"

Madame Destinée raised one finger to silence her. "It won't take but a moment. They won't notice a thing. I promise."

Madame Destinée retreated, and the door clicked shut behind her. Groans and disappointed sighs thickened the air, but that wasn't surprising. Lindsey imagined she'd be the same way in another two weeks.

"What was all the sniffing about?" She watched Ellie wrap a purple scarf around her neck. She still didn't smell anything odd, but Madame Destinée obviously had.

"This will sound strange, but that's how she knows who's ready for private lessons." Straightening up onto her toes and shoving her nose into the air, she waved her arm as Madame Destinée did. "*You are growing fruits, darlings. When the time is right, your talent will be sweeter than any other smell.*" Considering Ellie's accent, she did a great impression. "I told you it's strange."

Lindsey picked at the hem on her shirt. Madame Destinée was weird, but perhaps she meant it different than it sounded. "On TV there are dogs that can smell cancer. But I've never heard of a person smelling anything like that."

"Maybe Broussard smells it and pokes her with his nose?"

"Could be." But Lindsey doubted it. Talent didn't leave a scent. Plus, she hadn't noticed Broussard doing anything. She'd have to pay more attention next time to be sure. It sounded more like Madame Destinée was making it up. Or she thought it made her dancers try harder to get into the private lessons. Still, sniffing was a strange way to do it.

Ellie finished dressing and waved goodbye before she left. Lindsey didn't want her to go. Sitting alone in a room full of girls who didn't want to talk to her would be as fun as pulling bubblegum out of her hair. Trying to ignore the lingering whispers and stares, she pulled her legs up on the bench, wrapped her arms around her knees, and let her head fall forward. She was tired. Exhausted. She wished she could curl up in her sleeping bag and go to sleep.

"I don't like you."

The words pierced through Lindsey's fog. With a yawn, she looked up to find Adela towering over her.

"*Vete*. Go away. You don't belong here."

Lindsey refused to react. She was too tired. She hoped that if she ignored Adela, the girl would go away.

It didn't work. A tidal wave of Spanish hit instead. Lindsey didn't understand a word but was extremely impressed that Adela's tongue moved so fast. Whatever Adela wanted to say, she finished it quick. With a last *Hmpf,* she spun on her toe and headed out the door. As she swung it open, Madame Destinée's voice echoed from down the hallway.

"Lindsey, would you join me, darling?"

Lindsey stood and stretched her legs. They ached, but then so did the rest of her. At least she'd go home soon and finally get some sleep. As she went to the door, Adela blocked the space.

Lindsey yawned a grumble. It was too late for this. Stifling another yawn, she waved her hand and motioned Adela to get out of the way. "Excuse me. Madame Destinée's waiting for me."

Adela didn't budge. "I told you to leave. Go home. Never come back."

Building anger melted the last bit of foggy sleepiness away as Lindsey stared at the girl. Sometimes the dancers back in Nebraska were snotty or rude. It was something that belonged to competition and ballet, but never did any of the girls physically block someone. Judging by Adela's flexing fists on her hips, she'd be more than happy to throw a punch, too. Lindsey refused to back down, but there was no way she'd provoke Adela by trying to push forward, either. That'd make things worse, and she wasn't about to go there.

"Lindsey, are you coming, darling? I don't like waiting."

"Coming!" She called loud enough for the entire dance

school to hear and let her gaze settle on Adela. "Well?" The girl had to move if she didn't want to explain this situation to Madame Destinée. That conversation wouldn't exactly gain Adela bonus points.

Adela mumbled something under her breath but stepped away. Her glare sizzled on Lindsey's back all the way to the office door.

Inside, Madame Destinée stood by the shelves, holding one of the music boxes. She dusted the golden edges with her finger and whispered to the figurine. It wore a red, black, and gold costume like the one Sanae Aito had worn. With a tired sigh, Madame Destinée closed the lid and placed it on the shelf.

"Please, sit down." She rounded the desk and sat. Her shoulders slumped as if in aching pain.

"Are you okay?"

Madame Destinée gazed back. "Oh, it's nothing, darling. I was trying to lift Broussard and must have moved wrong."

Lindsey nodded. "My dad sometimes has that problem, too."

The wooden stool was warm, probably since Sanae Aito had just been sitting there. Lindsey wondered if she'd been accepted into the private lessons. She hoped so.

Another yawn had Lindsey gaping like a fish. "Sorry," she apologized.

"It is late, darling." Madame Destinée rubbed her hand over her head, right along a streak of white. The color contrasted with her otherwise black hair.

"I like your hair. It looks nice."

Madame Destinée's eyebrows shot up in confusion.

"The white stripe on the side of your head. One of the girls at my school back in Nebraska had one like that in pink. I tried to get Mom to let me have one in blue, but she wouldn't let me."

Gaze narrowing, Madame Destinée fingered the spot. "Ah, yes. That. Sometimes, it's nice to try something different, especially when embarking onto a new stage in life."

"Oh. Are you doing something new?" Lindsey wondered what it could be. Hopefully, she wasn't closing the dance school. That'd be a catastrophe. Before she could ask, Broussard darted out from behind the water dispenser.

Ruf. Ruf. He bounded up onto Lindsey's lap and licked her hand again and again, until it was covered in a layer of dog slobber.

"Broussard," Madame Destinée scolded.

"It's okay."

He buried his head against Lindsey's stomach, and she couldn't help but wrapping her arms around him. "Hey, Broussard. I heard you barking after the show."

"I think he's blushing." Madame Destinée stared at him with a loving smile before dropping into serious mode. "Your performance with Robert this evening took me by surprise. It's not often that two dancers share the same feeling for the music. A *pas de deux* usually takes years to perfect, but the earbuds together with the music unleashes hidden talents—another useful invention my brother left me. I would like you and Robert to dance together in tomorrow's show. Since Christmas wasn't long ago, I've been considering adding a scene from the Nutcracker, and now I have the perfect performers."

"The Nutcracker? Really?" Lindsey leaned forward, practically knocking Broussard to the floor. "Sorry, Broussard, but I love that ballet! I've always dreamed of dancing the role of Clara."

She would get to dance the role of Clara! Just thinking about it made all tiredness disappear. "Wait. You want us to dance it tomorrow?"

"That's correct."

Whatever excitement Lindsey felt dissipated. *Tomorrow.* There was no way she'd learn the choreography that fast, even if she spent every hour until the performance practicing it. And then to learn it with Robert. She didn't even know how to dance *pas de deux*, let alone master it with him in one day...and the new choreography. It was insane.

"I can tell by your face what is bothering you, but there's no reason to fret. I'm sure you've figured out the trick behind the earbuds already."

Lindsey squirmed. "No, not really." She did notice when the

music played that she hadn't cared about anything but dancing. It was as if she was caught in a dancing world. And afterward she felt wonderful.

"Come, darling, you must have noticed, especially since the performance ended with you and Robert performing a lift. Or had you practiced performing those with him already?"

"No." Of course not. Lifts like that took years of practice. She'd only met Robert before the show, which meant— "The earbuds did that?" It didn't seem possible. It didn't make sense, but if what Madame Destinée was saying was true, then the earbuds and music made her dance in a way she never could have performed on her own. "How do they do that?"

Madame Destinée stared at her, waiting for her to figure it out on her own.

"Hypnotism?" It was how the other music box worked, so it made sense. Kind of. None of it should be possible, but obviously it was. "Wow," she whispered.

Broussard wiggled to get out of her arms, and she realized she was squeezing him too tight.

"I'll take that as yes, you will dance with Robert tomorrow?"

"Yes. Sure. Thank you." Her voice sounded flat even to her own ears, but excitement bubbled inside her. Her thoughts stuck like sticky goo, unable to understand everything.

Madame Destinée laughed. "It is late. You should head home and get some sleep. I'm sure everything will be clearer for you tomorrow morning."

Lindsey nodded, but she was pretty sure that it still wouldn't make sense in the morning. "Do you want me to come here earlier tomorrow and practice all day?" She had no clue how she'd pull that off, but if it meant dancing as Clara in the next show, she'd find a way.

"Come when you can, darling. I'll be here."

After a nod, Lindsey gave Broussard a huge hug. She couldn't believe her luck. She would be dancing with Robert and performing the role of Clara. It was a dream come true!

"*R*ise and shine, sleepy head."

Mom's warm fingers brushed against Lindsey's cheek, but she didn't move. It was too early to get up, and the sleeping bag was so warm and snuggly despite the hard floor. Bridget's music whispering from the kitchen didn't call to a bright morning, either. It sung a sweet lullaby, perfect for dreaming.

ZISH! Lindsey peeked through one eye to see the top of her sleeping bag flap to the side, ripped away to let her freeze like an icicle.

"Aw, Mom. I'm tired." She pulled her knees to her chest to stay warm. "Five more minutes, please."

Bridget had rehearsals at 8:00 am, but that didn't mean Lindsey had to get up, too. It was still Christmas break.

A shadow fell across the sunlight coming through the window. "You look pale. Are you feeling sick?"

"No." The rest of Lindsey's words drawled into a yawn. "I'm…jusss…tired."

"Tired or not, it's a bright, sunny day. I've got to take Bridget to violin rehearsal, and then I'm heading over to the café. You can sleep after we leave, but I want to see you dressed and eating breakfast before I go. Oh, and Ms. Mulberry asked me to give this to you. She's such a sweetheart." Mom pulled a small red rose out of her pocket and tossed it to Lindsey before leaving the room.

The rose laid on the wooden floor next to Lindsey's sleeping bag. It was made of paper, carefully folded so that the rose petals stuck up. A little tab hung on one of the petals in the center with the words 'tug here.' It was cute, but considering it came from Ms. Mulberry, it screamed suspicious. She picked it up and stared at it from all sides before pulling the petal as the words instructed.

57

The rose unfolded. Inside, there was a message.

Roses are red, violets are blue, questions abound. I'd like to see you.

"What questions?" If Ms. Mulberry had any questions, she could ask Mom. Lindsey didn't see why she should go downstairs and answer them. After all, it was only Witch Mulberry's way of luring her in for a visit. Lindsey wasn't that stupid.

Tossing the note aside, she changed clothes and headed to the kitchen.

Bridget sat on a bar stool along the counter, stirring her spoon around a half-eaten bowl of cornflakes. Her violin lay in the open case to the side.

"I wish Mom would buy that chocolate cereal with the marshmallows in it." She took a long, slow slurp.

Lindsey plopped down onto one of the stools next to her and bounced a couple of times. The padding was cushy. "Where did the bar stools come from?"

"Dunno. I think someone at Dad's work gave them to him." Bridget jammed a spoonful of milk into her bowl, sending little splatters of white across the counter.

"You better clean that up before Mom sees."

"She knows I don't like cornflakes."

Lindsey stared at Bridget, unable to believe her ears. "Mom spends her whole day running around and cleaning up other people's messes at the café so you can go to Juilliard."

"So?"

"So, it wouldn't hurt you to do something nice for her and clean up your own mess."

Bridget shrugged and dropped her spoon in the bowl again, sending more milk splattering in all directions. After rolling her eyes at Lindsey, she picked the spoon back up for another bite.

That did it. Lindsey swept the bowl away from Bridget and slammed her hand down on the counter with a *splat.* "Who do you think you are?"

Bridget stared at her. The spoon hung half-way out of her mouth. "Your sister."

"My sister was nice. She wasn't a self-absorbed twit. Ever since you found out you'd been accepted to Julliard, you've become some self-serving queen. *Daddy,*" Lindsey held her hair up in two pigtails—as Bridget tended to wear them—and squeaked a horrible imitation of her voice. "*I'm going to Julliard because I'm SO special. We're moving to New York, and you can work a second job. Mom will work, too. All to pay for me. Oh, Lindsey? Who's that? You mean my stupid sister? She doesn't need friends. She doesn't need silly ballet classes. She doesn't need anything because it's all about me and me alone.*"

Lindsey panted. Her body shook from head to toe. Never had she been so angry. It had nothing to do with the milk, but it didn't matter. Bridget was getting everything, and she didn't care!

Tears welled up in Bridget's eyes. Her cheeks puffed up until the first tear fell.

Lindsey's fire dwindled.

"I'm sorry." Bridget's voice was small, so weak and lost. Her eyes glistened with a waterfall of tears. She tumbled forward and slung her arms around Lindsey's waist and buried her head in her sweatshirt. "I don't want to go to Juilliard, not without you. Why don't you go there? You can take my place."

Guilt oozed in Lindsey's throat. That's not what she meant. Of course, she wanted Bridget to be famous. But she wished she could be, too. *Ugh.* Wrapping her arms around Bridget, she pulled her close. She was so soft and small. "I'm sorry. I really am. I'm glad you're going to Juilliard. You have to go. You have to make it big someday. You have to do it for me."

Bridget eased away and stared up with big, chocolate-brown eyes. "What do you mean for you? That won't work. You need to be in the spotlight, too. You promised me, remember? We're supposed to be famous together."

Lindsey's throat squeezed tight. They'd made that promise to each other years ago, right after Bridget's first solo recital. She'd only been five. Lindsey was sure she'd forgotten about it. Obviously, she hadn't. Bridget still believed in her. Feeling the wet streaks slide down her own cheeks, Lindsey wiped the tears off with the sleeve of her sweatshirt.

"I have a surprise for you," she croaked.

Bridget's eyes bulged. "You do? What is it?"

"Something way better than soggy cornflakes. Tell you what, if you clean up the milk mess, I'll get it. Okay? On three. One... two...three!"

Bridget dove to the roll of paper towels while Lindsey dashed across the living room to her coat and pulled out the doughnut.

When she swung herself back onto the bar stool, the counter was spotless and clean.

"And? What is it?" Bridget pulled one of her pigtails around her head and chewed on the end.

"Here." Lindsey set the donut on the counter.

"A pink donut with colored sprinkles! You're the best sister in the world!" Bridget started to dive in for another hug, but Lindsey held her back and pointed at the donut.

"You might want to eat it before Mom sees."

One bite and half of the doughnut disappeared. "Did you get it last night when you snuck out?"

Lindsey froze. "What are you talking about?"

"I saw you sneak out of the house last night. Where did you go?"

"Nowhere." The answer slid out before she could think about it. Bridget had seen her!

"Liar, but I won't tell Mom and Dad. Promise." Bridget put down the donut. She grabbed her left earlobe with her right hand and her right earlobe with her left hand. "Cross my heart, hope to die, stick ten fingers in my eye." It was the most bonding swear they had, one that couldn't be broken even when faced with death.

"Fine." Telling Bridget wasn't a great idea, but Lindsey didn't see how she had a choice. One word to Mom and Dad, and her classes with Madame Destinée would be over. "I danced in a ballet. There's a school on the other side of the block, a really nice one, and the teacher is giving me lessons for free. All I have to do is dance in her shows every night."

Lindsey watched Bridget's expression carefully as it swept from a pucker mouth to a bumpy forehead to widening eyes with a humongous smile.

"Wow! That's amazing! Are you sure you don't want to tell Mom and Dad? I bet they'd want to come and watch you. I want to come and watch you. Can I?"

"Nope. No way. The shows are at midnight. Mom and Dad would never let me go if they found out. This is our little secret. Us sisters have to stick together." Lindsey stuck out her pinky for a secret sister sign, a special one they'd used once before when Bridget was five and had saved a kitten from drowning in a nearby creek. For three days, they'd snuck food out to it right under Mom's nose—cats made Mom's whole face swell up like a hot air balloon. The fourth day, the cat ran away, and they never saw it again. But that promise had never been broken. Not once.

Bridget hooked Lindsey's pinky in her own and sealed the shake. "Got it. But I still want to watch you dance in one of the shows sometime."

"We'll see." Which meant no because there was no way she'd ever let Bridget go out in the middle of the night with her. It was way too dangerous. Plus, Bridget was afraid of the dark.

"Are you two done with breakfast?" Mom's heels clicked from her bedroom.

"Hide the donut," Lindsey hissed.

Bridget rolled the rest of her donut inside the napkin. "I'm not hungry anymore anyway." She stuffed it into the trash can and climbed back onto the stool as Mom entered the kitchen.

"Everything all right? I thought I heard you two fighting."

"Us? Fighting?" Bridget wiggled her eyebrows at Mom, and then she cracked a stupid smile back at Lindsey.

"You girls are silly." Mom reached in for a duo-hug, but it ended too quickly. "Bridget, are you ready? We've got to get going or you'll be late." She tucked the loose strands of hair under her pink hat and tugged it tighter over her ears.

"Yep, I'm ready, ready, ready!" Bridget bounced off the stool with a gigantic leap. Giggling, she held her arms straight out. She spun around three times before dashing into the bedroom.

"Wow. She's in a good mood. Must have drank too much silly juice." Mom laid her hand on Lindsey's back and gave a gentle rub. "Your father's going to be an hour late today. Ms.

Mulberry told me she'd be thrilled to have you come over for a visit. She means it, too."

Lindsey thought back to the flattened paper rose still on the floor near the suitcase. A tiny speck of guilt poked her, but she shoved it away. She had better things to do than visit a cranky old woman.

"I'm sorry you have to sit around by yourself until he gets home. I wish—"

"I'm fine, Mom. It's not that bad here. Really," she added, seeing Mom's doubt.

Mom sighed, and with no warning whatsoever, leaned over and gave her a kiss on the head. The smell of maple syrup and bleach engulfed Lindsey as she inhaled.

"I know this has been hard on you. Your father told me that you two discovered a nice café. If you'd like, I'll take you there on my day off. Just you and me."

A smile snuck out, covering Lindsey's face. "Yeah, I'd like that." A lot.

After Mom herded a still giggling Bridget out of the door, the familiar *clunk-clunk-clunk* of the deadbolts sounded, reminding Lindsey that she had to get going, too. She snatched the extra set of keys from the top of the fridge, grabbed her coat—she wasn't going to forget that again—and waited ten minutes by the door before heading out.

The icy breeze, the smell of warm hotdogs, and the hum of traffic outside on the sidewalk felt familiar. To call New York home was still too much, but Lindsey could see herself living there. She stepped up onto the snow piled along the side of the street and balanced across the top. The packed ice was peppered with dirt and pebbles, not exactly slippery. Why some of the other people didn't walk that way was beyond her, but adults always thought they were too mature for such things. When she reached a spot where the pile was stomped down from people crossing the street, she leaped over it and landed on the sharp peak of ice on the other side on one foot. Without thinking, she stretched out into an *arabesque*.

Someone hooted. A few more people whistled and cheered.

Lindsey froze. She'd performed a *grand jeté,* and a huge one, too! Her cheeks warmed as more and more people stopped to see what was going on, all fingers pointing at her. It was embarrassing... way too much. Wanting to hide, she jumped to the sidewalk and ran as fast as she could around the corner and down the next block. Her whole body shook. What had she been thinking?

The door to the dance school stood wide open. Without stopping, she thundered inside and slammed the door closed behind her.

Madame Destinée waved from the end of the hallway with a tape dispenser clenched between her teeth. She stood on her toes, pushed the top corner of a poster against the outside of her office door, and stuck it tight with a piece of tape. After poking it a few times, she lowered onto her feet, took the dispenser out of her mouth, and stepped back to study her work.

"Perfect. Absolutely marvelous. What do you think?" She spun around. Her eyes widened as she took Lindsey in head to toe. "Oh my! You're flushed. Did you run the whole way?"

"I did a *grand jeté* over the snow, right outside on the sidewalk. I didn't want to, but my legs automatically sprang before I knew what I was doing. And everyone stared at me."

"Of course, you did, darling. I told you that my methods bring out your true talent. And you are very talented. Believe me. Here, I want you to see this. It's quite fitting that you should be the first to see it." She waved her arm in a majestic arc through the air and ended with an elegant pose to present the poster hanging next to her. The woman on Mom's favorite game show couldn't have done it better.

Lindsey went to read the poster, which wasn't hard. It covered the entire window on the office door—big and blue, a nice midnight blue. Madame Destinée's red-lipped smile beamed in the center of it. The cool gray stripe in her hair wasn't there yet, but she still looked like a model. Above her head sparkled these golden, swirly words:

Dawn of a New Era

"Isn't it lovely? In two nights, I will take the stage and give the performance of a lifetime. Right at midnight on New Year's

Day. The last thirty years I've hidden in the shadows. It gets so tiresome, darling, not having an audience adore me. But now the waiting is over. I will again be on the stage."

"I thought you already danced in Rome, Berlin, and London."

Her smile soured worse than vinegar. "How do you know about those performances?"

"Someone told me." Suddenly, she was sorry she mentioned it. Not that she knew why it was a problem. There was nothing wrong with dancing in a performance. Unless Madame Destinée didn't want her students to know for some reason, which seemed to be the case.

"Who claimed that?"

"I dunno. I think one of the other dancers said that. But I don't remember. I may have misunderstood." Telling by her glare, it was best to make the whole topic go away fast and mentioning Mr. Lagunov would not do that. It'd lead to more questions. "They speak so many different languages. I don't understand anything."

"Ah, yes. Language can be a difficult barrier." Her smile returned, brighter than before. "Do they say anything about me?" She moved closer as if expecting a row of secrets.

"Well..." Slices and pieces of what Ellie had mentioned about Madame Destinée somersaulted past. There wasn't much. "Barely anyone speaks English. But they love dancing here, and everyone hopes to get into the private lessons." That much was true. But the memory of Adela's sneer flashed though her mind. Lindsey shoved it away. She wouldn't mention that. Dancers never played nice when it came to competition. Even in Nebraska, a girl would pour hand lotion in another's shoes or *accidentally* trip someone when they went on stage. Not everyone did things like that, but there were always one or two. Madame Destinée had to know that, too. It belonged to ballet like fluff to tutus.

Madame Destinée touched her lips. Her fingernails sliced across her red lipstick. "That is lovely. They are dying to share their talent with me."

The way she said it chilled Lindsey. She tugged at her coat against the goose bumps growing on her arms.

"I...I better get going. I have to change." Without waiting

for a response, she hurried down the hallway and into the warm changing room. The heat there didn't help. She wrapped her arms around herself and stared at the empty room. She was overthinking things and probably imagined the strange way Madame Destinée had said those last words. Or maybe it was because Madame Destinée worried about her own upcoming performance. Anyone would be nervous.

It was weird that Madame Destinée didn't want anyone to know about her other performances. When Lindsey had mentioned the ones Mr. Lagunov had told her about, Madame Destinée acted like they were to be kept a secret. Since she was holding her own performance in the next few days, there was no reason to hide the other ones. But then, she said she wanted the audience to adore her. Maybe the other performances weren't going well, and she hoped this performance would change things around.

Lindsey let out a puff of air and leaned her head back against the wall. Thinking about it gave her a headache. But at least Adela wasn't there. That was something.

Forcing all of her thoughts aside, Lindsey slipped into her leotard and tights, and plopped down onto the bench.

A metallic *clunk* echoed through the room.

Instinctively, she shot a glance over at the doorknob. It turned.

"Hello?" she asked.

There was no answer, but the knob didn't release, either. Someone was there. She gripped the edge of the bench. Her fingernails stabbed the wood.

The door opened.

Slowly.

"Hello?" Her voice squeaked.

The door paused, but she couldn't see anyone through the crack. The only thing that came was a long, howling moan.

*C*rash.

The door burst open. A large shape bounded into the changing room.

Lindsey screamed...until she saw the intruder and his gigantic smirk. "What are you doing?" She snatched up a nearby pair of balled socks and flung them at Robert's head.

He caught them with one hand. "Whoa! And I thought I was uptight."

She squeezed her clothes tight around her chest, wishing her face wasn't heating up. "You almost gave me a heart attack."

"I did?" He smiled a second, raised his arms above his head, and clawed his fingers into what Lindsey guessed was supposed to be a werewolf impression, and growled. "GRRRRRR!"

She rolled her eyes. "You're not that scary, you know."

"Your scream sounded pretty scared to me."

"This is the girl's dressing room. I could have been, you know, dressing?" It might have been the truth, but it was a lame excuse. They both knew she'd freaked.

With a shrug, he plopped down next to her. "Madame Destinée wants us to wait for her here. Huh, I've never been in a girl's changing room before." He sniffed. "Doesn't stink as bad as ours. Oh, by the way, Madame Destinée wants you to eat this." He pulled a small, pink cake in a baggy out of his pocket and placed it on the bench next to her.

Lindsey stared down at it. Half of it was squished. It didn't look as delicious as the cakes the day before.

"All okay?"

Lindsey nodded and slid farther away, still not sure what to think of him. After all, he had barged into the girl's changing room and was now sitting beside her. Awkward didn't even describe it.

"I see you're one of those girls who needs to defrost first. Got it." He cleared his throat. "Let's start again. My name is Robert. I live in Boston with my mother, father, and one older brother Kurt. I have a cat named Greg, who's never around, and my favorite color is green. Now, it's your turn."

"Did they all come here with you?"

His eyebrows lowered in confusion.

"To New York. Did they all come with you?"

"Oh, so you don't know." The way he said it, like a fact everyone knew but her, irritated her beyond belief.

She slid farther down the bench.

He slid after her. "Everyone who dances here comes from different countries, but you noticed that. Strange thing is, they are physically in those countries right now. They are coming to this dance school without leaving their homes in other places around the world."

She shook her head. No, she didn't understand. He babbled more nonsense than Ellie.

He paused, obviously seeing her disbelief. "I'm not lying. Or crazy. Trust me, I know it's a massive, sci-fi brain trip. One of the guys who was here before thought it might be a portal of some kind. Madame Destinée's brother was a genius. He must have invented a machine that transports people around the world. ZAP! Just like that." He snapped his fingers and grinned.

Lindsey shook her head. "Come on. That's impossible."

"You obviously don't know much about Jeannot Broussard. He was amazing. A true genius. He made all sorts of cool toys that could move and speak, like robots but more natural, as if they were alive. And none of them used computers or electricity or anything like that. Pure mechanics and detailed work. He was so ahead of his time."

"Huh." She hadn't heard any of that before. But even if Jeannot Broussard had done that, it didn't mean he'd made a transport device. No one could do that...could they? It made her head hurt more trying to imagine it.

"So, you live in New York?" he asked.

"We just moved here...there...well, to New York. My little sister Bridget is an amazing violinist and was accepted into Juilliard. She's only eight." Lindsey puffed up a little. She loved saying that.

"Wow. That's impressive! So, Madame Destinée found you in New York."

"Her school is...or a door to the portal is..." She squinted up at him, questioningly, but when he tilted his head without comment, she continued. "...down the block from our apartment."

Placing his arms behind his head, he leaned back. "She found me about a week and a half ago. I was on my way home from hockey practice—"

"You play hockey?" The picture of him in a helmet and carrying a hockey stick didn't work, not after seeing him in his ballet costume. It'd be like Romeo pretending to be the Hulk on ice. It didn't fit.

"Yeah, I'm the official bench warmer. I don't get to play much. Kurt's the real athlete. He's team captain." He stared down at his hands and pushed his knuckles together. "He makes me feel useless. Not that he rubs it in or anything. Everyone expects me to be as good as he is because I'm his brother. Hockey's supposed to be in the blood. Guess I got the wrong blood."

"Don't be stupid. I can't play the violin. I tried. It was terrible." Even the memory of the screeching made her cringe. "But I can dance, and Bridget can't. She has two left feet. I bet your brother can't dance."

Robert snorted. "Yeah right, as if I'd be geek enough to ever let him know I dance ballet."

"Your family doesn't know? How did you take lessons all those years without them noticing?"

"Lessons? I didn't even think about dancing until Madame Destinée found me. Trust me. It's not something guys usually want to try. Men in tights—that's not real manly."

"You don't look bad in tights." The small voice came from the doorway.

Lindsey glanced up to see a person dressed as bright as the sun coming in.

68

"Ellie." Robert shot her a cool chin nod, and then he nudged Lindsey with his elbow again, but a purple scarf smashed over his head. Next came a familiar balled-up pair of socks. "Hey, what's that for?"

"For being in the girl's dressing room." Ellie smiled at herself and plopped down on the other side of Lindsey. "You took ballet before Madame Destinée found you?"

Lindsey nodded. "Back in Nebraska. And Broussard found me." She couldn't help but smile at the memory.

"He's a cute dog," Ellie confirmed.

"With a rotten name." Robert picked up the balled-up socks and tossed them up and down with one hand. Judging by the side-glances he was throwing Ellie, she was going to get bombarded. "Who names their dog after their dead brother? That's creepy."

"He's still cute." Ellie leaned back, making sure Lindsey's body shielded her from a possible sock attack.

Not wanting to land in the middle of a war, Lindsey snatched for the socks from Robert but swiped air. His smile made her grumble.

"I have one of Jeannot Broussard's music boxes at home. Grandma gave it to me for my birthday last year," she said, deciding to ignore him.

"That box must be valuable," Ellie said.

Robert leaned forward, kneading the socks in deep concentration. "Does it do anything strange?"

"Uh, no. Should it?"

He shrugged. "Maybe..."

The girls waited for him to say something more, but he just sat there squishing the socks.

"Maybe what?" Ellie finally asked.

Reaching up, he fiddled with an amulet hanging around his neck. "All those music boxes in Madame Destinée's office give me the creeps." He shuddered.

"I know what you mean." Ellie let out a sigh and slumped back against the wall. "Last time I was in the office, there was a box on the desk with a figurine wearing the same outfit as Sanae Aito. I wanted to cry when I saw it, although I don't know why.

It's only a music box."

"I went into Madame Destinée's office right after Sanae Aito had been there. It gave me goose bumps." Lindsey shuddered at the memory.

"The whole thing is weird," Robert said. "I went into Madame Destinée's office twice last week. Both times after she'd sniffed the best dancers out and called them in." He clutched the amulet tighter in his hand. "I swear, the figurines looked like those guys."

"You mean their costumes were the same," Lindsey corrected.

Robert shook his head. "The one guy I'd talked to quite a bit, and he had this mole on his cheek. Right here." He poked at a spot not far from the corner of his mouth. "The figurine had a mole in the exact same place."

"Are you sure it wasn't dust?" Ellie asked.

Robert snorted. "Yeah, right."

"What do you think it was then?" she asked.

"What do I know?" Robert shrugged. "I'm just telling it how it is."

Lindsey shivered and hit his shoulder. "You're trying to freak me out again."

"Maybe." Robert held the smile only a second more before letting it die away as his stare concentrated down onto the amulet in his hand. After a moment, he tugged it over his head. "Here." He stabbed it out toward Lindsey. "Take this."

She gazed over at him, not wanting to take it. "It's yours. I don't want it. Why would you give it me?"

"I'd feel better if you took it." He grabbed her wrist and held it while he laid the amulet in her hand. "Madame Destinée has her eye on you. Everyone's noticed it."

A warm hand settled on Lindsey's leg. "He's right. I don't like the way she looks at you. Like..." Ellie bit her lower lip as she considered something.

"Like Lindsey's a juicy hamburger," Robert said. "With a side of fries. Never forget the fries."

"That's not true. She didn't even sniff at me last night." Lindsey shoved the amulet back at him, but Ellie reached over and stopped her.

"Yes, she does. It's creepy."

"And this will help how?" Lindsey studied the blue amulet. In the middle of the stone, a ring of white surrounded a circle of light blue. In the center, a black dot stared back at her like a pupil. It reminded her of a round eye.

"It's called the evil eye," Robert explained. "My uncle brought it back for me from his vacation in Turkey last year. All tourists buy one. It's supposed to ward off evil."

"What kind of evil?"

"Well, the green-eyed monster anyway." He poked her arm and chuckled.

Lindsey rubbed her arm and tried to glare as if it had hurt, but her smile gave her away. "So, there are monsters I need to watch out for?" She leaned back, curious to hear his list.

"One big one. Jealousy. That's what it guards against," said Ellie. "I'm from Europe. I've seen the evil eye before."

Since there was no way to win the argument against them, Lindsey pulled it over her head.

Robert's arm drew back. Lindsey ducked to avoid the socks. They barely missed her head.

"Hey," she grumbled.

Ellie caught them with as much finesse as Robert had. "My brother plays American baseball." She winked. "I think these are Adela's. We could—"

"Let them go for a swim in the toilet!" Robert jumped up, but before he could retrieve the socks from Ellie, the door screeched open.

An icy draft rushed into the room—cold and prickly. Lindsey gripped the amulet tight in her hand when Madame Destinée appeared.

"Robert, Lindsey. Are you two ready?"

Robert and Lindsey followed Madame Destinée into the hallway. She pointed to the stairway at the very end, which led to the stage.

"The others are practicing in the studio, so I'm taking you two directly to the stage. It will help you get a better feel for the performance tonight."

Lindsey followed behind Robert. When they reached the stairs, she stopped. Something wasn't right. The staircase didn't look the same as it had before. The banister stretched up like an old skeleton. The rails hung crooked in all directions. Whatever gold Lindsey had seen lining the steps before must have been a reflection from the lights because there were only rusted nails now.

"Are you coming or not?" Robert asked.

After a moment's hesitation, she stepped onto the first stair.

Creak. Lindsey flinched. It was déjà vu.

When she stepped up to the next stair, it didn't creak. It cracked, threatening to break. Lindsey quickly bounced up to the third, her heart speeding up as she stared at the stairs above. Some looked half-decent—they'd probably be okay—but others yawned with gaping holes. One wrong step, and they'd break.

"Something wrong?" The stair creaked again when Robert joined her.

Lindsey's knuckles whitened as she clutched the railing. It didn't make sense; the stairs had been perfect. They'd shimmered and gleamed. How they had turned into Horrorville overnight was beyond her.

As the next stepped cracked, about to give, she jerked to a stop. No way was she going to continue climbing them. It'd be committing suicide!

Robert spun around and tilted his head. "You coming?"

"Nope. I'm not ready to die yet." She eased down again, watching the stair below carefully as she shifted her weight. She wasn't going up those stairs. No way. Robert rolled his eyes and bolted up the staircase. The boards cracked as he sprang over three steps at a time. About half-way up, he grasped the railing and swung himself through the air. The support beam cracked and wobbled under his weight.

Lindsey's heart hiccupped. "Stop! You're going to hurt yourself!" She dashed up the stairs, avoiding the holes as best she could. Her fingers snagged his wrist, and she yanked him back from a bending beam.

"Ow!" He knocked her hand away and rubbed his wrist. "Gosh, you should be on our hockey team. Kurt would love to have you slam those guys into the walls. What's your problem anyway?" He studied her for a moment. "Don't tell me you're scared of heights."

"Huh? No, I'm scared of falling to my death." She pointed at the huge gaping hole right next to his feet. "Since when is that safe?"

He stared down at where she was pointing and shook his head. "I don't know what your problem is. I like the gold edging. It makes the staircase look like it belongs in a castle, don't you think?"

"Gold edging? You don't see the hole?" It was right there. He had to see it. It was as big as her foot!

He cocked his head to the side. "You sure you didn't knock your head against the wall when I scared you in the changing room?"

"I do not have a concussion if that's what you think. The hole is right there." Lindsey bent down and poked her finger through it. He had to see that even if he was hallucinating. Wood never let fingers pass through.

His face did twitch for a second, but the reaction disappeared as quickly as it'd come.

"Are you coming, darlings? We don't have all day." Madame

Destinée's call rang sweet as sugar.

"Come on." Robert grabbed her hand and tugged her to his side. "I don't know what you're scared of, but I promise I'll get you up these stairs. I'll protect you with my life." He added a wink and pulled her up the rest of the stairs. At the top, he didn't pause but tugged her through the backstage room and out onto the stage.

"We made it. See. I kept you safe."

Lindsey pursed her lips to argue, but the two spotlights beaming from the sides had her blinking to see. As her eyes adjusted, she finally glimpsed the rest of the theatre, and it was not what she expected.

The chairs weren't as fancy as the ones in the first row. Except, the first row didn't look anything like it had during the performance either. The red cushions were gone, leaving worn wooden seats. The armrests didn't shine with polish. They were falling apart.

"Isn't it amazing?" Robert gripped her fingers tighter.

Lindsey choked. Amazing was not the word she'd use to describe it, nor would any other rational person. Something was wrong with Robert's eyes. Or hers. "What do you see?"

He gave her an odd look but played along. "There are rows and rows of chairs. They have red, velvet cushions with gold strings along the edges. They look soft enough to sleep on."

"Oh." She was afraid of that. One of them wasn't seeing things right. Except they were standing there together. It didn't make any sense.

None of it.

"Are you okay?"

She stared down at the bulge where the amulet hung beneath her leotard. It warmed more than before. Or that could be her imagination, too. "Yeah. I got dust in my eyes. Everything is blurry. Just give me a second. It will be okay." She wanted to tell him what was really going on, but something told her he wouldn't believe it. She didn't want him to think she was completely crazy.

Robert reached up, his mouth opening to say something, but before he spoke, Madame Destinée came over and pushed an earbud into each of their hands.

"It's time, darlings."

The music started and lifted them away. The stage blurred into a mass of clouds filled with music. Lindsey's feet danced across the floor, letting the rhythm guide each step. As the music slowed, she bent over and felt a hard surface push against her from behind. She sat on a chair, and something tickled her toes. When she glanced down into the colorful clouds, she saw a pair of pointe shoes embrace her feet—perfect sky blue.

She rose, *pliéd,* and *révéléed en pointe* with Robert right there. Together, they danced across the stage. The shoes enabled Lindsey to flutter as light as butterfly wings.

When the music stopped, she was poised in a dive over Robert's head. The move should have been beyond their capabilities, but there she was, arched to perfection with him supporting her with one arm.

"Okay. Whoa," she gasped, but before panic could sink in, he swung Lindsey down to her feet.

"See? I'm stronger than you think."

She rolled her eyes as he flexed his arm muscles. "All I see is chicken filet."

"Hey, these filets—"

"Bravo! Bravo! That was splendid, simply marvelous!" Madame Destinée pranced onto the stage, clapping as she hurried to join them. "The audience will be overwhelmed when they see you tonight." Her smile widened until it was as big as Bridget's had been when she opened her Christmas presents a few days before. "You two must be starving. I wouldn't want my stars to be too weak to perform. You should join the others at the buffet downstairs."

Lindsey turned to look back out into the theatre, but Madame Destinée grabbed their arms and tugged them backstage. "Come on, darlings. Oh, and Lindsey, I hope you enjoy your new shoes."

Without waiting for a reply, Madame Destinée waved her arm over her head in an arch, danced toward the stairs, and leaped down with a smile, but her toes headed right toward a broken stair.

"Madame Destinée!"

Lindsey scrunched her eyes, unable to watch, but at the last moment, the woman spun a twirl and slid around the hole with death-defying grace. Lunging and leaping, spinning and twirling, every hole and crack slipped by as if she were making careful moves across a board game.

Robert cleared his throat. "So, you have new shoes?"

Lindsey forced herself to turn her gaze to her feet. "Yeah. Pointe shoes. They should hurt since I've never worn them before, but they don't. They usually take weeks to break in."

Her toenail still hadn't fully grown back from the first pair she'd worn months before. She'd only worn them for a few weeks—she'd been so excited to finally get a pair! But then, her feet decided to hit an unexpected growth spurt. The ballet instructor insisted Lindsey wait a couple of months before wearing a pair again.

She moved her feet from one side to the other and studied the shoes. They were pretty, but it was odd they didn't hurt. Not that she was complaining. Nobody liked pain.

"They feel as snuggly as my fuzzy bunny slippers," she said.

"Come on then, fuzzy bunny." Robert grabbed her hand and started to pull her toward the stairs.

Lindsey planted her feet. "Oh no. I'm not going anywhere near those stairs." But she still needed a way to get out of the theatre. "I'm taking the front entrance." She turned to march back to the stage, down through the theatre, and out the main doors, but Robert rushed behind her and grabbed her wrist as she reached the edge of the stage.

A smirk tugged at the corner of his mouth. "I know a faster way."

Before she knew what hit her, he swept her up into his arms and vaulted down the stairs. The boards creaked and snapped as he bounded down two stairs at once and paid no attention to the holes every time he landed. Lindsey gripped him hard, closed her eyes, and prayed they wouldn't get hurt.

When her feet touched solid ground, her knees wiggled like jelly, and she leaned against the wall.

Robert laughed. "Oh, come on. It wasn't that bad."

A crack came from a stair near the top of the staircase. A piece of wood plummeted through the air and hit the floor a few feet away. Lindsey jumped. Her heart beat double time. That fate could have met them!

"Problems, darling?" Madame Destinée stood a few steps away. Her gaze scorched Lindsey.

It was the same look Mom had given her once when she'd been caught sneaking a peppermint out of Dad's secret stash in his sock drawer. But this time, Lindsey hadn't done anything wrong. Still, Madame Destinée's glare made her squirm.

Robert bounded up next to her, slung his arm around her shoulders, and gave a tight squeeze. "Nope. No problems. I was helping Lindsey overcome her fear of heights."

"Heights is it?" Madame Destinée cocked an eyebrow but let it lower into a stony glare. "Lindsey, now that your knight has come to your rescue, I'd like you to go into the dressing room and inform Adela that she is to come to my office as soon as she's done changing. After that, you will join Robert in the dance studio and *eat*. I found your cake untouched on the bench. I hope that won't happen again." A piercing squeak cut the air as Madame Destinée spun on her heel and marched to her office.

Robert let his arm fall away from Lindsey's shoulders. "Somebody sure takes their cake seriously. Everything all right?"

"Yeah." Lindsey crossed her arms tight over her stomach to keep them from shaking.

Robert reached around her neck. At first, she started to back away, but as soon as his fingers gripped the band, she let him tug the amulet out from beneath her leotard. Grabbing her hand, he brought it up and pushed the amulet into her fingers. Without a word, he continued toward the studio.

Lindsey rubbed the amulet as she watched him disappear, wondering at the gesture. When he was gone, she released a huge breath. Every part of her ached. Too much stress Mom would say, although Lindsey didn't know if that was true. She did know she wanted to go home and crawl into her sleeping bag. With the covers pulled tight over her head, she'd pretend she was back in Nebraska. Back in her blue bedroom with a window that overlooked nothing but cornfields and a blue sky.

Holding on to that thought, Lindsey straightened and marched toward the changing room.

"What do *you* want?" Adela's sneer hit like a wall the second the door opened.

Lindsey didn't flinch. It wasn't as though she expected rainbows and sunshine from Adela. "Madame Destinée wants you to come to her office." With the message delivered, she turned to head right back out of the room.

"Come to me, my love! Hurry, hurry! You can't keep Robert waiting." Sloppy sucking noises, which Lindsey guessed were supposed to be kisses, followed her out the door. "*Te amo mi amor!*"

Lindsey balled her fingers into tight fists and pushed them hard against her sides. *Argh!* Never had she met anyone as irritating as Adela! If anyone qualified to be classified as a witch, it was her. An ultra witch. Storming down the hallway, Lindsey shoved through the door to the dance studio and, without thinking, let it bang shut.

Absolute silence hit.

Half a dozen dancers stopped and gawked at her as if she were a monster charging into the room. Wrapping her arms around herself and wishing she could make herself disappear, she hurried around the line of food tables and ducked behind a mound of French fries.

"You survived." Robert stood there already stuffing his face.

"Barely," she grunted.

"Adela again?" Ellie came up from the other side with a strawberry perched in each hand. "Forget it. Dumb question. Of course it was her."

"There's only one thing to do with someone like that." Robert spun around and fumbled with something on his face. When he turned back, two fries dangled out of his nose. "Stuff fries into her face!"

"Ew! Gross! Are you a two-year-old?" Ellie and Lindsey swatted at him; Ellie's strawberry left red marks on his arms.

He ducked out of the way, headed around the table, and ran smack dab into a dark blue chest.

Lindsey choked.

"Madame Destinée." Robert swiped the fries out of his nose, dropped them to the floor, and kicked them under the table.

"I see you're enjoying yourselves, darlings."

Lindsey quickly straightened, but Madame Destinée didn't even glance at her. Her gaze was locked on Ellie.

"When you're finished here, come to my office."

Ellie nodded, but Madame Destinée had already turned to the other dancers. "Almost ripe," she muttered. "And Lindsey?"

Lindsey twitched. "Yes?"

"I see you still haven't eaten anything. Do that. Now." With that, she pulled open the door and left.

As soon as the door closed, Ellie clutched Lindsey's shoulder and tugged her closer so she could whisper into her ear. "This might sound crazy, but I'm not sure I want to go."

"Why not?" But Lindsey knew the answer. Since the conversation in the changing room, the thought of Madame Destinée's office and her music boxes sent instant chills running down her spine. She reached up and grabbed the amulet, wondering if she should give it to Ellie instead.

Before she could decide, Robert's arm sunk down around her. "Talking about me?"

Lindsey leaned away to shake him off, but he shifted closer to Ellie instead.

"If you don't want to go into her office, then don't," he said.

Ellie's mouth dropped. "You wouldn't go if you were me?"

He let go of Lindsey and rubbed his neck. "I'd say 'no', but it'd be a lie. When she calls me, I'll go. That's why I'm here. But I'd still be nervous about it. Sometimes, Madame Destinée weirds me out. I guess you should trust your gut—or that's what my dad always says." A smirk pulled at his lips as he swung up his arm and pulled her in for what appeared to be a painful hug. "No matter what you do, I promise never to throw your socks into the toilet."

With a roll of her eyes, Ellie elbowed him lightly in the

stomach, and he let go.

"So, what are you going to do?" Lindsey agreed with Robert. The music boxes were creepy. And that with the stairs and stage was beyond strange, but Mr. Lagunov had said that Madame Destinée was known to recognize which dancers had talent and which did not. She'd discovered some of the greatest dancers in the world. It'd be stupid to give up on a chance like this, no matter how unexplainable some things were.

Ellie must have had similar thoughts because determination now erased all doubt from her face. "I'm going. I want to take Madame Destinée's private lessons. That's why I'm here. And soon, both of you will be joining me."

"That's the attitude. Now, go on, and we'll see you again in those private lessons." Robert gave Ellie a gentle shove toward the door.

"Right, I can do this."

Taking a deep breath, Ellie marched across the studio. At the door, she hesitated and waved at Robert and Lindsey. As soon as Ellie disappeared, doubt poked again. Lindsey wrapped her arms around herself and stared down at the red strawberries. Red on a golden platter. Red, black, and gold—the colors of Sanae Aito's dress.

She picked one up and turned it in her hand

"You've got a pickle face again. What's wrong?"

She bit the berry, and the juice instantly tingled over her tongue. "Do you think there will be a music box with a figurine wearing Ellie's costume on Madame Destinée's desk right now."

"Probably." He grimaced but then tossed a French fry into his mouth and moaned. "Gosh, these are good."

Lindsey popped the rest of the berry into her mouth. It was so sweet! The flavor tingled and bounced until she couldn't help but smile.

"What were we worried about?" Robert chomped down another fry.

Lindsey shrugged. She had no idea, although she knew that there'd been something. But she didn't worry about it. If it had been important, she wouldn't have forgotten.

"Watch this!" Robert bounced on his toes and popped fry after fry into his mouth.

Lindsey laughed. It was funny. He was bouncier than a rubber ball.

"I bet I can jump even higher."

Lindsey giggled while she watched him. The tingles rolled down her throat and into her stomach, tickling her from the inside out as they went. Robert was amazing! He stretched and shrank with each bounce with the grace of a rubber band. It was hilarious...impossible.

Lindsey reached down for another strawberry. Now that she had eaten one, she realized how hungry she was.

"I love Madame Destinée's food." Robert bounced around behind her almost banging against the wall. "Every time I eat it, I feel great!"

Lindsey's fingers froze. It was the food. She jerked away from the table, her eyes glued to the berries. The tingles. The giggles...

"Lindsey, look!" Robert pulled on his face, forcing it into crazy positions as if his skin was made of putty and not flesh and bone.

Sparkles danced along the edge of Lindsey's vision as the happy tingles inside of her again grew. She clenched her hands into fists and stared at the floor. She had to fight the feeling. Whatever it was, it couldn't be right. As she watched the wooden floorboards, their color shifted from brown to sheer gold.

"No. No." She closed her eyes and shook her head, trying to chase the impossible sights away, but when she opened them again, the entire room glistened and shone.

Like the staircase.

Like the theatre.

"Laugh and play, my Lindsey!" Robert danced around her, bopping up and down. Back and forth.

He lifted another fry to his mouth.

Lindsey slapped it away.

"Hey, what was that for?" His bouncing stopped, but a goofy grin gleamed. "A new game?"

81

"Don't eat any more. There's something wrong with the food."

His eyes crinkled for the span of a heart beat before seriousness melted away. He reached forward, grabbed her hands, and tugged her closer.

"Lindsey! Lindsey! Dance with me, my Lindsey!" He sang and hopped, tugging her along with him.

"Stop," she begged. "Stop!"

He froze. Instantly. His eyes sparkled with a million stars as if a container of rainbow glitter had spilled inside of them. "You are my Lindsey. You are my girl." His voice was soft and confused.

She stared at him, so close. A new wave of tingles hit her gut, different than those from the strawberry. These tingles were more squirmy and wiggly. They didn't make her want to laugh at all.

She swallowed and shook it down. "The food messes with our heads. You've got to fight it."

His gaze locked onto hers. Behind the stars, clarity broke through. "The food?"

She gripped his arms. "Yes, the food. Those tingles make us see things that aren't there. Everything looks better than it is. Like the staircase."

"Madame Destinée." Robert pulled away; his grin was gone. He rubbed his hand through his hair and took in a deep breath. "That's why you were acting funny before?"

"Because I didn't eat the cake." And that's why Madame Destinée had been so angry when they'd reached the bottom of the stairs at the end of their practice. She knew that Lindsey had seen the truth. The school wasn't beautiful or grand. It was a dump.

"But why?" Robert asked.

Lindsey shook her head. She had no clue. "It might be her pride. She doesn't want us to see how awful everything really is."

When Robert didn't respond, she looked up to find him staring into space with a huge grin. A fog coated his eyes. "Robert?" She grabbed his arm, willing him to come back to her. He was the only one who knew. "Robert, don't."

"Ah, Lindsey!" He snatched her wrist and tugged her around into a duo-spin. She fought to keep from stumbling as he dragged her to the center of the studio, swerving in and out of the other dancers.

The moment he paused, she shoved him away. "Stop! You can fight it. I know you can."

"Nope. I don't want to. You think Madame Destinée's school is a dump. That she's too embarrassed to show it. But that doesn't make sense. Look at how beautiful it is?" He spun around, his arms wide to hint at the entire studio. "Which leaves one possibility. You are a snob." He dabbed her nose with his finger. "Snobby, snobby, Lindsey."

Throat tight, she gazed up. "What?"

"You are a snob like Adela."

"No, I'm not. How can you say that?" She knew it was the food talking, not him. But it still hurt.

"You're right. You're not like Adela. My Lindsey is nice and pretty." He reached forward to grab her again.

She stepped back and stumbled smack-dab into one of the French girls.

"*Oui*. A snob!" She giggled as she moved out of the way.

"Snob!" screamed another boy from across the studio.

"Snob! Snob! Snob!" The chorus raged in from all sides. The dancers stopped whatever they were doing and came toward Lindsey, taking one step with every word.

"Snob! Snob! Snob! Snob!" The chanting grew faster and louder. Closer and closer. And in the center of them all came Robert.

"Let's dance, my snobby bunny."

Shaking her head, she backed away. "No. Don't. Robert." But he kept coming forward, step after step. Arms open wide.

Finally, she couldn't take anymore. Spinning around, she dashed out the door and into the hallway. Tears fogged her eyes, and she gulped for air as she fought not to cry. But she couldn't help it. The tears already ran down her cheeks. She watched the door to the studio, hoping no one would chase after her. When it remained closed, she leaned against

the wall and dropped her head into her hands. *Snob.* How could
he say that? They were friends. She knew it was the food, but
still, couldn't he fight it? She had. The giggles were long gone.
Now all she felt was pain. Betrayal. If Robert wanted to...if he
was her friend...he would have tried to fight it, too. But he didn't.
He called her a snob.

She snorted against the tears, wishing she'd never come to
the school. Everything about it was wrong—the music boxes, the
earbuds, the food. Even Ellie would no longer be there. It didn't
matter if Lindsey became the star of the show because she had no
one to share it with.

She was alone.

Snob. The word echoed in her head again and again. And it
hurt so badly.

"Lindsey?" Madame Destinée's voice was muffled and far
away. "Is that you, darling?"

Lindsey rubbed the tears from her cheeks. She couldn't let
Madame Destinée see her like this. The woman had wanted her to
eat the food. She'd see right away that Lindsey wasn't happy. But
the more she scrubbed away the wetness from her face, the more
the tears came. She wished she could run away and disappear.

Madame Destinée stepped out of her office and saw her.
"Darling, are you crying?" The wrinkles on her face deepened
as she hurried forward. "What happened? You should be in the
studio enjoying the food with everyone else."

"I don't feel good. My stomach hurts." The excuse always
worked with Mom.

"Oh, you poor thing! We can't have you getting sick, not
with the big show tonight." She flicked her wrist and held out
four tiny cakes. "Here, take these. They'll help. I promise. Then,
you can go home and rest. You'll need your strength for tonight.
And you don't want to miss the performance. You are going to be
the star of the show."

Lindsey stared at the cakes as Madame Destinée dropped
them into her hand. She managed not to cringe. No way would
she eat them. Never again. She wanted to throw them away. But
she couldn't, not with Madame Destinée towering above her.

"Yes, ma'am." She gave a weak smile.

"Hurry home, darling. I need you at your best."

Lindsey nodded, turned, and shuffled down the hallway. As soon as she was outside and several stores down, she tossed the cakes onto the street and stood there refusing to move until a truck drove over them. When the cakes splatted into a mush, she let go of a breath she hadn't realized she was holding.

They were gone. Good. There was no way she would ever touch any of Madame Destinée's food again.

That night Lindsey lay in the sleeping bag, waiting for Dad to flush the toilet one last time before he went to bed. He always did. Every single night.

"When are you going to leave?" Bridget's voice exploded against the silence.

"Shh! Aren't you asleep yet?" That explained why she hadn't heard Bridget snoring.

"Don't you have a show tonight?"

Lindsey didn't answer but rolled over in her bag to stare at her music box a few feet away on the floor. The lid was open, and the figurine's yellow skirt glowed in the moonlight. Yellow like Ellie's but not as puffy. Not as happy and bouncy, either. *Ugh.* She hoped Ellie had made it into the private lessons. Or maybe it was better if she hadn't. Maybe it was better if Ellie was as far away from Madame Destinée and the dance school as possible.

"When are you going?"

Bridget still wasn't asleep. Of course not.

Lindsey flopped her head against her pillow. "11:40." She wasn't sure she wanted to go, not after what happened that afternoon. Not only didn't she know what to think of the food but sitting in the changing room without Ellie would be a nightmare. Lindsey swallowed against a knot building in her throat. *Snob.* She couldn't face any of them ever again.

"Do you have friends there? I haven't found any at my school yet." Bridget's voice hung soggy and sad. "They're all on Christmas break."

Lindsey flipped over and watched Bridget's silhouette sitting on her sleeping bag. She fidgeted with her hair.

"Is that why you can't sleep?"

86

"Dunno."

Guilt poked her. She hated to see Bridget upset, even if she was getting everything. She was still her little sister. "Are you scared you won't find any new friends?"

"It's like you were telling me once about ballet dancers. Everyone wants to be the best and becomes jealous and mean. There aren't many kids my age who get into Julliard. I don't think they'll like me."

She knew what Bridget meant. And it stunk. It was like with Adela. She was a super dancer. There was no reason for her to be a jerk to everyone. Talk about a low self-esteem. It was stupid. "But there are always nice people, too."

"Yeah. Right." Bridget sniffed but didn't seem to be crying. At least Lindsey hoped she wasn't.

"Do you have friends?" Bridget asked.

"Yes...or I thought I did," she whispered the last part too quiet for Bridget to hear, but the words stung. Lindsey clutched her sleeping bag as an empty ache grew in her chest.

Snob.

"Can I meet them? When I come to see you dance, I mean. You said I could."

Lindsey's head snapped up. "No, not yet. I've only been there a couple of days. You've got to wait until I learn the steps first." Big fat lies draw the most flies, or that's what Grandma always said, and Lindsey could hear the buzzing in her ears from the one she had just spat out. But there was no way she could let Bridget come anywhere near that school. Not until she figured some things out first.

Bridget's shadow slumped. "Okay. I get it."

Lindsey let out a breath, and her whole body relaxed. She reached up for the amulet and wrapped her fingers around it. It was warm like Robert's hands when he lifted her into the air.

Robert. Her perfect dance partner.

Her friend.

Even if he'd said those terrible things, it wasn't his fault. The stupid food messed with his head. He didn't really think she was a snob. He couldn't. She refused to believe it. And as a friend, she wasn't going to leave him. She had to warn him about the food again. She had to try.

Reaching up, she grabbed her alarm clock. 11:30 pm. It was early, perfect. If she got there early, she might be able to find him when he came into the school. And she had to find Ellie. Ellie needed to know about the food as much as Robert did. *Ugh.* If Ellie was still at the school—and Lindsey hoped she wasn't—she had no clue where to look for her.

She inhaled a lungful of air, shoved the mumble-jumble in her head to the side, and got to her feet. "I have to get going."

"Break a leg," Bridget said.

Lindsey snuck over to her parents' room and placed the tiny music box on their floor. After tapping it three times, she hurried to the kitchen and grabbed the keys.

Shadows darkened the staircase more than usual, and the air hung thick with silence. Everyone, including the witch, slept. Lindsey tiptoed down until she reached the main doors.

Creak. The noise came from the stairs above.

Clankity-clankity-clank. A metallic jingle echoed through the stairwell.

Not waiting to see who it was, Lindsey dashed outside.

On the sidewalk, she didn't stop running until she was several buildings down from her own. Silence clung to the streets more than before. The clouds blocked out the moon, and several street lights were out, making it hard to see anything. She wrapped her scarf tight around her neck.

Snap.

Lindsey spun around. Looking at the dark street leading back to the apartment, she dug in her pocket for the alarm Mom had given her. A piece of paper blew out from between parked cars.

Crash.

Lindsey screeched. That was not paper!

As she gripped down to push the button on the alarm, a white cat sprang out from behind a pile of boxes. They stared at each other for a second before the cat darted over the sidewalk and disappeared into the row of parked cars.

"Dumb cat."

She started to turn, but something else shifted in the shadows, something larger. It appeared to be a person. He or she stood hidden behind the boxes. Eyes glistened in the lamplight and locked right on her.

Lindsey turned and ran. Her heart thundered in her head. The buildings and street around her blurred. When she reached the corner, her boots skid on the ice, causing her to stumble and slide, but she managed to stay on her feet and make it to the dance school's door. Not daring to see if she was still being followed, she hurried through the door. The pictures rattled along the walls as she slammed the door behind her and pressed her back hard against the glass. Gulping, she fought to catch her breath.

"Lindsey, is that you, darling?"

"Yes." Her voice cracked.

"Will you join me in my office for a moment?"

Lindsey pushed her balled up fingers against the brick wall and forced herself to calm down. She didn't have time to talk to Madame Destinée. She needed to find Robert before he ate the food.

One breath...

Two breaths...

Lindsey shoved whatever fear she could to the side as her breathing calmed. There was no way to avoid Madame Destinée, but maybe it was better that way. Now, that Lindsey stared down the hallway, she realized she had no idea where the boy's changing room was. Madame Destinée did. All Lindsey had to do was get her to tell her where to find it.

Madame Destinée sat in her office behind her desk. A silver picture frame glistened between her hands. "Darling, I'm glad you're here. Is your stomach feeling better?"

Lindsey took a deep breath and clutched her hands behind her. They still shook. "Much better." She'd say whatever Madame Destinée wanted to hear...anything to find Robert.

Madame Destinée set the frame on her desk and slid it to the side, leaving the picture at an angle. The man portrayed in it wore thick, black glasses. His gray hair stood up in all directions as if he'd stuck his finger into a light socket. He wore a fancy tuxedo with a bright red bow tie. It matched the shiny red apple in his hand. Lindsey wondered why anyone in a tux would have their picture taken with an apple.

"You know him." Madame Destinée pushed the picture across the desk so Lindsey could get a better look.

"I do?"

"Of course. He's my brother."

"That's Jeannot Broussard?" Lindsey leaned forward and pulled the frame all the way to the edge of the desk. His smile warmed.

"It was taken shortly before he disappeared. A nice photograph, don't you think? He adored apples."

With a small yelp, Broussard sprang out from behind the water dispenser, dashed around the desk, and bounced up, making Lindsey fall into the chair. He snuggled against her stomach. The smell of soap hung on his fur, and he was puffier than before. Even the dark rings around his eyes were brighter.

"You had a bath." She buried her nose in the powdery smell. It was warm and comforting.

90

Madame Destinée glided her fingernail along the edge of the desk. "May I ask you something personal?"

Lindsey's gaze shot up. "Uh, I guess."

"I spoke with Robert this afternoon. He mentioned you have a sister."

"Bridget," she said carefully.

"A lovely name." Madame Destinée leaned forward across the desk. "I understand that she's a talented little girl, quite like yourself. She attends Julliard at eight years of age?"

Lindsey nodded. "She plays the violin." The queasiness Broussard's fur had erased came rushing back. Bridget wasn't a dancer, so Madame Destinée shouldn't care about her. But the gleam in Madame Destinée's eyes made Lindsey's stomach churn.

"I thought Bridget—" she pronounced Bridget's name one syllable at a time "—might like to watch you perform in tomorrow night's show."

"But I thought I'm not supposed to tell anyone—"

"Oh, no, darling, I never said that. It's probably better if you didn't mention anything to your parents, that's true, but sisters are completely different, especially those as talented as yours."

Madame Destinée's eyes flashed with something which Lindsey didn't understand, but it made her skin crawl. She'd never let Bridget come here. Not a chance.

"Now that we've settled that, I have something else I want to talk to you about. I promised that you and Robert would dance in tonight's show, but I'm afraid we're going to have to cancel that."

Lindsey gulped so fast she nearly choked. "What? Why?"

"You needn't pull such a sad face, darling. It has nothing to do with you. In fact, I've decided to let you dance a solo. You'll be the Sugar Plum Fairy."

"But what about Robert?" She pressed her hand against her coat where the amulet rested.

"It appears his family has little understanding of the fine arts. I'm afraid they won't let him take lessons from me anymore. Did he tell you about their inexplicable interest in hockey?"

Lindsey didn't reply. Of course, he'd mentioned the hockey

problem, and now he was really gone. Just like that. There was no reason to warn him about the food because she'd never see him again. She held Broussard tighter and could feel his heart thudding steady and true.

If Robert was her friend, he would have said something. That's what friends did...if he'd truly been a friend.

Snob. His voice echoed in her mind, stabbing more than before.

"Then, you understand his problem." Madame Destinée rose from her chair and went to the shelves. "A pity. You and Robert danced so well together. I would have loved to have you both in my show again."

Lindsey pressed her hand against the amulet, the evil eye. Robert had given it to her because he was concerned about her. He was her friend. She could feel it in the depths of her gut. There was no way he would have left without saying goodbye. She didn't believe it.

Madame Destinée sauntered down the row of shelves until she reached the music box at the end. The lid was still open.

The figurine wore a costume like Robert's.

A shudder raked through Lindsey, and Broussard shifted in her arms. She forced herself to remain calm. "Can I see that music box?"

Madame Destinée tilted her head a moment and then shrugged. "I suppose." She brought the box to Lindsey and placed it in her hands.

The figurine wore a violet outfit. Its dark hair had been painted in a sweep to the side.

Robert.

"You two danced well together."

Tears dripped down her cheeks as she stared at the figurine. It was wooden. Lifeless. And it looked so much like him.

"I think it's better if we put it away for now." Madame Destinée reached to take the box from Lindsey, but Lindsey held it to the side.

"I'll put it away." It seemed wrong to let Madame Destinée touch it again.

With a nudge, Lindsey convinced Broussard to hop back to the floor. She kept both hands around the box as she stood and made her way to the shelf, but she didn't look at the figurine as she went. She couldn't. It hurt too much.

When she reached the spot where it'd been before, she set the box carefully on the shelf and finally peered at the figure again. It was amazing how much it resembled Robert.

Madame Destinée came up behind her and reached over her shoulder to close the lid. Just before the lid swung shut, the figurine winked.

"Wait!" Lindsey reached for the box, but before she could move, Broussard darted right past her feet. With high-pitched barks, he bounced back and forth across the office so crazed Lindsey might have thought his tail was on fire.

"Calm down, boy. What's wrong with you?" She bent down, and he immediately sank back on his haunches and let her scratch between his ears.

Madame Destinée perched her arms on her hips. "Broussard! Behave yourself."

With a sad whine, he balled up next to Lindsey's feet and tucked his muzzle underneath his paws.

"I'm sorry, darling. He's overly excited about tonight. He can't wait to see you dance. He's your biggest fan, you know." Madame Destinée strode past him, shaking her head. Behind her desk, she eased into the chair. "Well, darling, you better get going. You still need to get changed for the show."

Lindsey's gaze shot up.

"You're going to be the star tonight. That hasn't changed."

"Oh. Right." A performance without Robert. The thought made her feel empty.

Outside the office, the hallway stretched, dismal and dim. Each of Lindsey's steps trudged. She knew she should be happy; tonight, she'd be dancing a solo. She'd be the star! But she didn't want to dance. Not without Robert. She was alone.

Robert.

His figurine had winked. *Didn't it?* She shook her head, trying to shake the image away. Figurines didn't wink...couldn't wink.

93

A chill flowed over her skin when she pulled the door open to the changing room and let it *thunk* closed behind her. Robert's figurine played in front of her mind, winking again and again. It was impossible. But the more she thought about it, the more she was convinced it had.

Her mind buzzed as she let her feet guide her to the bench. All she could see was that wink as she snatched up her leggings and tugged them on.

If it did wink, what did that mean? That she was going crazy?

"We need to talk."

She looked up. *Adela.* As if things weren't bad enough. "What do you want?"

Smoothing her dance skirt, Adela eased onto the bench. "I'm sorry I was mean. I know you won't believe me. But I was wrong. *Lo siento.*"

Lindsey's thoughts stuck like old bubblegum. "Okayyyyy..." Adela would never apologize. No way.

Lindsey shifted on the bench, trying to work it through her head. She didn't believe a single word. But ignoring the apology wouldn't work, either. Adela *might* actually mean it. Probably not, but still. With a puff of air, she finally nodded. It felt as though she was giving in to a poisonous snake, especially when Adela broke out into a grin.

She reached out to hug Lindsey, but she must have seen Lindsey flinch because she pulled back again. Her smile continued to hold as bright as a spotlight on the stage. "Since you're nice, I'll tell you something. Your friend, Ellie, is in private lessons. I saw her."

"You did? That's great!" Or was it? Ellie wanted it so badly, and Lindsey wanted to cheer for her. But that meant she still had to warn her about the food.

"You are worried?" Adela's forehead furrowed.

Lindsey stared up at her, not believing Adela was truly concerned. But that wasn't her biggest worry. "You saw Ellie, right? Do you know how I can find her?"

"She has lessons in the studio after our show."

"At one in the morning?" That sounded awfully late.

Adela shrugged. "*Si.*"

"*Pardon.*" One of the French girls, the one who had looked up at her before, stood a few feet away. She held her hands folded in front of her. Her eyes were soft. Kind.

She shifted. "You and Adela...uh...*l' amie?*"

"Friends." Adela nodded, grasped Lindsey's hand, and held it tight in hers. "*Si*, friends."

Lindsey wanted to pull her hand away but knew she couldn't. Calling Adela and her friends wasn't quite right but denying it would be worse.

"We all friends, no?" Adela reached up and grasped the French girl's hand, too.

The French girl nodded, slowly at first but quickly added a smile.

"All of us, *si?*" All around the room, girls nodded, some more hesitant than others, but Adela's burst of excitement beamed out as if she were a light bulb. Even Lindsey had to admit it was contagious.

"I'm so happy! Now we celebrate."

Adela dropped her hands and charged across the room to her pile of clothes. She dug out a small plastic bag and sprang back toward Lindsey with the biggest smile on her face. "Here." She held the bag out to her. "You are first. My mother bought them this morning. They are my favorite. *Saladitos*—salted plums."

Lindsey forced herself not to flinch. Salted plums? But the French girl was smiling, so it was impossible to break the flow. Going with it, she took the bag. "Thank you."

The ends of the bag were glued shut. The bright red label displayed a cartoon llama which had a huge, toothy grin. Along the top, the word *Saladitos* beamed over the llama's head—store bought and unopened. Lindsey mentally poked herself as she realized how closely she was investigating the bag. Thanks to Madame Destinée, she'd probably never view food from other people the same way again.

A wave of salty-sour air gushed out when she opened it. The brown-white clumps were the size of walnuts and looked like dried up balls of mud. She touched one. It was as hard as stone.

Adela leaned forward. Her eyes glistened wide and expectant. The French girl already reached out a hand for one.

Deciding it couldn't be too bad, Lindsey popped a *saladito* into her mouth. *Ew-yuck!* It was like eating a tablespoon of salt!

"Do you like them?"

She pushed her lips together, forcing herself not to make a sour face, and nodded with a smile that felt twisted and knotted. But it held.

"And me?"

Lindsey pushed the bag toward the French girl faster than she probably should have, but nobody noticed. The girl snatched out a plum, tossed it into her mouth, and rushed the bag to her friend. Soon, everyone in the room was eyeing the brown balls or fighting back puckered faces as they popped them into their mouths.

But Adela remained rooted in front of Lindsey.

"Thank you," Lindsey said.

"No, I thank you." Adela's smile tightened and curled as a sneer settled in. "Madame Destinée will be happy. Since you've eaten, I can go into her private lessons. I am her favorite now."

Tiny tingling bubbles spread across Lindsey's tongue. Familiar tingles. She spit the *saladito* out into her hands, but it was too late. The happy tingles pranced down her throat, bouncing around inside. They demanded she be excited, thrilled.

She balled her hands, fighting against it. She didn't want the tingles to take over. How dare Adela do this to her!

The girls around the room began giggling and laughing thanks to the plums. Lindsey didn't get it. She couldn't be the only one who noticed what happened when they ate the food. Why didn't anyone care?

Anger boiled inside of her, numbing the happy tingles until all she wanted to do was scream.

"What is wrong with you guys?" Her voice echoed between the walls. Everyone fell silent and stared at her. Normally, she would have died of embarrassment and wanted to crawl under the bench to hide, but not this time. She was done with all of it.

"Don't you realize the food Madame Destinée gives us isn't

okay? It makes us laugh and see things that aren't there. It's a lie. All of it. This entire dance school is a lie! There's nothing great about this school. Stop eating her food and you'll see it. The place is a trash heap!"

"Why do you say that?" Adela stood in the center of the room with her hands on her hips. She would have appeared meaner if the edges of her lips didn't constantly twitch toward a silly grin.

"It's true. Don't eat anything. Just once, and you'll see."

The room became deathly still. The other girls held their breath, but only for a moment. One giggled. Then the next. Soon the entire room filled with cackling laughter.

Tears formed in Lindsey's eyes as the joyful tickles broke through her anger and overpowered it. She wanted to laugh, giggle, and dance.

She wanted to cry.

"What's with Ellie?" she asked. "Was that a lie, too?"

"*Idiota.*" Adela snorted a laugh and strutted like a model across the room before sitting down to straighten the ties on her shoes.

Lindsey slugged back to the bench. The sugary explosions shoved her toward a blissful fog. She couldn't stop them no matter how hard she fought. But why fight? The world was wonderful! How silly she was to be mad.

Madame Destinée came into the changing room and clapped her hands. Everyone lined up at the door. Lindsey skipped to the end of the line, giggling the whole way. The changing room was bright and colorful with lights twinkling above like stardust.

They filed into the hallway and hurried to the stairs. The steps no longer only gleamed gold but also sparkled with diamonds. The polished wood glistened as bright as expensive crystal. The entire banister shimmered with silver and gold sparkles. Lindsey slid her finger over the railing, so excited she was sure she would burst. Tonight, she was a ballet princess. Tonight, the audience would beg to see her dance.

After parading up the stairs, they stopped in the backstage room. The air smelled sweeter than the honeysuckle bushes behind Grandma's house. A bottle on a box caught Lindsey's attention. For a moment, she recognized it. Robert's perfume.

Robert.

There was something about him, but she couldn't remember what.

Finally, Madame Destinée pulled back the curtain and waved them onto the stage. The lights above beamed bright as a sun. The audience grew silent, and the music played. Lindsey hovered across the floor *en pointe*. Her toes never touched the ground. She spun and twirled, flying through the air like a bird. When she came down, the amulet bumped against her chest.

Robert. He wasn't there to catch her. They were supposed to dance *pas du deux*. They were supposed to dance together.

But he'd left. He was no longer there. Neither was Ellie. They were both gone.

Another wave of silly tingles washed across her. She bounded back up, and her feet moved faster than before. Arms stretched, chin high, she drifted with the music—one *pirouette*, two *pirouettes.*

The music ended. She slumped forward, and her heart pounded in her ears.

"Bravo! Bravo!" The entire theatre shook. The audience cheered.

Madame Destinée nodded from the side of the stage and waved the other dancers to move away.

Lindsey closed her eyes and extended her arms. *Relax your fingers, keeping the middle one and the thumb close enough together to hold a candy cane*—she was graceful. She was the Sugar Plum Fairy. The muscles in her legs and feet tightened as she shifted into third position.

The lights were so bright they swallowed the audience into the darkness past the edge of the stage. It was Lindsey's time to shine.

The world glowed around her, and she sucked it in. She would dance, and the audience would cheer.

They would adore her.

The lights dimmed.

But Bridget wasn't there. Neither were Mom and Dad.

The music began, but Lindsey's feet remained frozen.

No one in her family would see her perform.

"Dance, darling," Madame Destinée called from somewhere beyond the fog as pink dust blew in Lindsey's direction.

The particles glimmered. When they reached Lindsey, her blue wrap skirt shone brighter, turning into a white, fluffy tutu with tiny pink beads. Silvery-pink shimmered on her leotard. Even her pointe shoes went white. She was worthy of the Royal Ballet.

Ruf. Ruf. Ruf.

"Broussard!" Lindsey peered at the darkness beyond the stage. She squinted to see him as rows and rows of cushioned chairs lining the theatre from back to front came into view. Broussard wasn't sitting in any of them. Nobody was. The entire theatre was empty.

Her breath caught as panic set in, but it disappeared again under a cloud of happiness. So, what if it was empty? The audience loved her. She could hear them cheer!

A pretty glisten in the middle of the rows of seats caught her eye. She squinted harder, wishing she could make out what it was. Something wonderful, no doubt, like the rest of the theatre. And then she found it. Right in the middle of an especially large chair sat a music box. Seeing it made her heart cry.

"Dance, darling."

The music drifted in from around the stage, engulfing Lindsey's every thought. As the joyful cloud settled in, her feet took control and glided across the stage.

"And one, and two, and...no, darling! You must hold your hands high above your head like a bird soaring through the clouds, not like a rotating sledge hammer!"

Lindsey forced her arms higher, bringing her fingers into a graceful arch. She felt like a human rubber band stretched so high. To make it worse, the floor below her rotated. Round and round until she was dizzy.

"Good! Now, hold it. Perfect!" Madame Destinée leaped around, clapping and dancing from one foot to the other. "That's gorgeous, darling, just the way it should be. You are so talented. So talented! This is what I want. This is the talent I need!"

Lindsey stretched higher and higher. Her muscles screamed in pain.

"Now, your toes, darling. You must stretch up as high as you can."

Her ankles popped as she straightened them, but she wanted to be better. She had to get it right.

When Lindsey couldn't stretch anymore, a sweet numbness coursed through her. It was a perfect pose! She peered at her toes, making sure they were poised to perfection, but when she looked down, her joy shattered.

The pointes were glued to the top of a rotating, metal pin—a music box pin.

Lindsey opened her mouth to scream, but her jaw wouldn't budge. It was shut tight. She tried to move her arms and legs, but everything was frozen. Stuck. Panic took over, and she screamed again. This time, it came as a weak echo inside her own throat. Her heart went silent in her ears. Her lungs refused to rise or fall. She was stuck. Unmoving.

A lifeless figurine.

Madame Destinée stepped up to her, and her twisted grin grew bigger and bigger. The rest of her grew, too, and soon she towered like a New York skyscraper. Her Statue-of-Liberty-sized nose hovered miles above Lindsey.

"Tomorrow, you will dance for me again. Tomorrow, you will be mine."

Lindsey wanted to scream. To run. But she was a wooden figurine. Stuck silent and trapped forever.

The world plummeted around Lindsey as Madame Destinée lifted her into the air and gently set her on a shelf between two other music boxes. One was yellow. The other violet.

Ellie.

Robert.

Another music box caught Lindsey's eye, one that still stood on Madame Destinée's desk. It was unlike the others—brown and carved with a hint of golden paint.

So sad.

So lonely. But tears couldn't come from painted eyes.

"Good night, my darling." Madame Destinée reached up behind her and snapped the lid down over Lindsey's head.

"Mom!" Lindsey bolted up. Her heart pounded and sweat coated her body, making her pajamas sticky.

"Mom!" She stumbled to her feet. The first ray of sunlight shone through the single window in the bedroom, warm and calm. She glanced up at the light bulb still hanging from the ceiling. The smell of Mom's morning coffee hung in the air.

Crumpling back down onto her sleeping bag, she hugged herself as tears rushed down her cheeks. It had been a dream, a nightmare.

"Bridget?" Lindsey's legs still shook. She desperately needed to hear her sister's voice, anything to reassure her that everything was okay.

"Bridget?"

The room remained quiet. Too quiet. Bridget's snoring didn't rattle the walls.

"Bridget?"

Lindsey flipped up onto her knees and scrambled toward the mound of Bridget's sleeping bag. She grabbed what she was sure was Bridget's shoulder but hit pillowed softness.

"Bridget?" Panic gripped but soon faded as a ray of sun brightened against her hand.

She was being silly. It was morning. Bridget was awake and probably eating breakfast. With the corner of the sleeping bag, she wiped the tears from her face and headed to the door. It was a wonder Mom hadn't yelled at her for not getting up yet. The door burst open before she got halfway there.

"Lindsey, what on earth is going on?" Mom stared over at her.

"I'm sorry. I had a nightmare, but I'm all right. Sorry, I should be up already. Is Bridget eating breakfast?"

Mom's eyebrows twisted into confusion. "Who?"

"Bridget."

Mom studied her for a moment. Lindsey wrapped her arms around herself again. Something wasn't right.

"Lindsey, your father and I are worried about you. I was willing to let it go. After all, the move is a big thing. But it's getting to be ridiculous. You're much, much too old to have an imaginary friend."

Lindsey stared. "What? I'm talking about Bridget. You know, my sister? The violin genius?"

Furrows grew across Mom's forehead. "Oh, Lindsey. I'm afraid we're going to have to take you to the doctor to get professional help."

Lindsey stepped back as Mom reached out to hug her. Bridget wasn't imaginary. Why was Mom saying that?

Mom's scowl melted and gave way to a silly grin. A goofy one that Lindsey didn't like at all.

"Mom?"

"Oh, I know what will help. One of our new neighbors brought by a box of cakes this morning. They're perfect for breakfast, a real energy bringer. They're on the kitchen counter. Why don't you go have one? Your father even ate two before he left."

"Cakes?"

Mom shrugged. Her smile ate up her entire face. "Your father found the box with a note that read 'From your neighbor.' They're so pretty. So sweet."

"I thought you said New York was dangerous. Why are you eating cakes from someone you don't know?"

Mom laughed. Loud and giggly. All wrong. "I'm in a hurry, and I've lost my keys again. Those funny keys. They always run off on me." With the wave of her hand, Mom twirled around and headed back into the hallway.

Uneasiness sent a shiver down Lindsey's spine. *Madame Destinée.* It had to be. Lindsey could recognize those stupid giggles anywhere, and they did not fit with Mom. Mom's laughter echoed from the living room, sillier and happier than it ever should have been, caused by Madame Destinée's cakes, no doubt. But why? Why would she bring them to their apartment for Mom and Dad to eat them?

She went to chase after Mom but tripped. Bridget's teddy bear looked up at her from the floor with its bright, green plastic eyes. Mom had called Bridget an imaginary friend, although the evidence was right there.

"Mom! Wait!" Lindsey darted to the hallway as Mom pulled the door shut. The three dead bolts clunked before she could get to the door.

Heading back to the bedroom, Lindsey snatched her clothes and got dressed as fast as she could. She had to hunt Mom down and talk to her.

"Lindsey."

Lindsey stopped with her arm stuck half-way in her sweatshirt. A voice called from somewhere in the bedroom.

"Lindsey."

She jolted around, but there was only the wall behind her.

"Lindsey, down here."

It was a tiny voice with a gentle ring.

Gazing down, all Lindsey saw was her music box. The lid hung open, and the figurine stood directly in a sunbeam.

Blue painted eyes blinked.

She fell to her knees. "You can talk." It was impossible.

The figurine's head tilted. "You must stop Madame Destinée. You must..."

Its face froze, wooden and lifeless.

"Hello? Hello?" The chimed music began to play, and the tiny ballerina jerked forward in her constant spin.

"Wait!" Lindsey bent closer. Her nose nearly touched the figurine's. "You said I should stop Madame Destinée. Please, help me."

The ballerina turned and turned.

"Please," Lindsey begged again. She wished it'd say something...anything.

She sat there until her legs went numb, but still, nothing came. Finally, she closed the lid and slid back against the wall, grabbing her pillow to hug it tight against her chest. The figurine had talked! She hadn't been dreaming. It was real. She was sure of it.

She stared at the closed music box. Her mind jammed, unable to process anything. Not that she knew what she should think. Everything that happened should have been impossible. But it was happening.

Lindsey felt limp and tired, as if she'd danced a marathon. If only she could close her eyes and wake up to find herself in Nebraska again. She sucked in air. But wishing wouldn't change anything. It wouldn't bring Bridget back.

Bridget. She had to find her no matter what.

Not sure what she was going to do but knowing she had to do something, Lindsey snagged her coat and went to fetch the keys from the fridge. Her fingers rubbed across an empty surface. "Of course," Lindsey mumbled. Mom had said her set of keys was missing. She'd taken the spare.

Not locking the doors would probably get her cleaning duty or house arrest, but Bridget was so much more important than that. She closed the apartment door behind her and headed down the stairs. When she reached Witch Mulberry's landing, she stopped. The door handle turned, but for once, Lindsey didn't run. Planting her feet, she faced the door and waited.

The door creaked open, but instead of a wicked witch, a pair of rosy cheeks and friendly eyes appeared. "Hello, Lindsey. Were you coming to visit me?"

The mole wiggled on the woman's face as she held the door wide open. "You're looking for your sister."

Lindsey's mouth dropped. "How do you know that?"

"I think it's time you came in, Lindsey. We need to talk."

The apartment was set up like the one her parents rented above, but wallpaper with red roses covered every wall. Ms. Mulberry waddled as she moved into the living room and headed toward a round table with an off-white tablecloth spread over it. The tablecloth, chairs, and nearby couch were all embroidered with tiny red roses. Lindsey would have thought the room should smell like roses too, but it stunk of moth balls and lemon cleaner.

"Go on, sit down. My legs can't stand forever."

While Lindsey pulled out the chair and sat on the rose printed cushion, Ms. Mulberry went to a shelf and pulled down a thick, heavy book. It *thunked* on the table as she laid it down. When she opened it, a cloud of dust drifted into the air.

After a cough and a sneeze, she settled down across from Lindsey. "I'm glad you finally came to visit, although I wish you would have come sooner. Didn't your mother give you my message?"

Lindsey fidgeted in the chair at the thought of the cute folded rose. Okay, maybe it wasn't a curse after all. "Yeah," she whispered. It was amazing how heavy guilt weighed, enough to make her want to slide under the table and right out the door.

"No worries. Things are as they should be. Everything carries a purpose and a time. Such as your family's move upstairs and your running across Madame Destinée."

Lindsey pulled her gaze away from a rose on the tablecloth. "You know her?"

"Of course. She was my apprentice once, long ago." She leaned forward, placed her elbows on the table, and cradled her face between her hands. "But I want to talk about you, honey. You see, you are destined to defeat a witch."

106

Lindsey flinched. "A witch?"

If Ms. Mulberry hadn't sat there looking like the most sweet and friendly person in the world, Lindsey might have gotten up, politely excused herself, and dashed out of the apartment before she could spell b-a-l-l-e-t. But Ms. Mulberry was nothing as she had been that first day, when she'd sat on the stairs on that folding chair. She was soft and kind, a lot like Lindsey's own grandma.

"You're sure?"

"No doubt about it." Ms. Mulberry leaned back. Her face beamed, although her smile dimmed. "Madame Destinée has your sister, and you were heading out to get her back. It's a good thing you stopped here first. I can't imagine what would have happened otherwise. Defeating witches can be a nasty business." She said this so matter-of-fact and calmly, as if pulling a splinter from a finger fit in the same category—a perfectly normal event.

Lindsey nodded slowly. Her hands slid tight under her thighs as they began to fidget. "How do you know all of that?"

She chuckled, the sort of laugh that made everyone in the room want to smile. It was similar to Madame Destinée's tingles, but this joy sprung from the heart and comforted like a warm hug.

"For one, I found a box of small cakes in front of my door this morning with a note claiming they were from your parents. But I knew whose magic had touched them."

"She gave you cakes, too?" Wow. Madame Destinée was going all out. The thought didn't make Lindsey feel any better.

"Silly of her, but she probably didn't realize I live here." She clicked her tongue in a light *tsk*. "She's always had a knack for magic, but she lacks discipline, and that's what has gotten us into this mess. If only I'd paid more attention. Mr. Lagunov warned me. He's such a wonderful man."

"You know him, too?"

"Didn't your mother tell you? I'm the one who suggested you go to his classes."

Lindsey nodded. Now that she thought about it, Mom had said that.

"The classes at the Community Center aren't the most impressive but make no mistake, if you have talent, he'll spot it and take you to his professional studio downtown."

"He has a professional studio?" The image of professional dancers bounding around to the song "YMCA" played in front of her mind, leaving her speechless.

"Let's stick to defeating witches first."

If it meant getting back Bridget, Lindsey agreed. That's all she cared about.

Pages rustled and snapped as Ms. Mulberry shoved the open book closer to Lindsey and jabbed her finger at a photograph.

"That's Madame Destinée."

Lindsey leaned forward for a better look.

"Years ago, I helped design costumes and a stage prop or two. I had a little talent when it came to making things shine." She winked but didn't pause long enough for Lindsey to react. "That's when I met Madame Destinée, a lovely woman with an amazing nose at spotting talented dancers. So many of those dancers she found went on to great careers thanks to her. But that wasn't enough for her. She wanted to be on the stage herself. Her brother, harboring his own talents, made a machine that enabled her to dance."

Lindsey bit her lower lip until it hurt. After seeing all the strange things in Madame Destinée's dance school, she wondered if anything was impossible.

"Soon, she could dance and held her own debut. Every chair sold out. When the music started, she was amazing…beautiful. But after a few minutes, her talent died. She tripped and stumbled over her own feet. The arrogant audience did the worst thing—they laughed. Madame Destinée collapsed. Her brother carried her to her dressing room and waited until the ambulance arrived. When they came into the room, he had disappeared and was never seen again. Madame Destinée never recovered from that night and fell into a horrible depression. Shortly after that, she died."

The book shut with a *thunk,* making Lindsey jump.

"She's not dead." Lindsey stared straight into Mulberry's eyes. "You just said she brought the cakes."

"Of course, she's not dead. I might have believed it myself for many years if there weren't rumors of her appearances in

Europe. I never expected to find her here in New York. But there's no doubt. I felt her presence several days ago, and those cakes have her magic all over them. I should know. I gave her the knowledge she needed to create them."

A sudden glint of fire shone in Ms. Mulberry's eye, and the helpless Mrs. Santa Claus disappeared. She was the woman on that folding chair, not a person to mess around with. Lindsey squirmed. If Ms. Mulberry taught Madame Destinée how to make the cakes, then Lindsey couldn't trust her, either. Still, Lindsey wanted to trust her. She seemed so…nice.

"Oh, now that's a lovely object!" Ms. Mulberry jumped up and leaned over the table. She swiped Robert's amulet from Lindsey's chest with her thick fingers. "The evil eye and a strong one, too! I can feel the magic in it. Perfect." She patted it back into place and plopped down into her seat.

"Use that. Understand?"

Lindsey nodded, and then shook her head. "No, not really."

"Oh, that's fine. It is a lot to take in at once, but we don't have a choice. The most important thing for you to remember is that jealousy is dangerous and should never be underestimated. Madame Destinée was able to find you because the two of you are similar...and your little sister, by the looks of it. Those who already possess great talent have no right to be jealous of someone else. Not that anyone ever has the right to be jealous. But that's what made you and Bridget so easy to catch."

Lindsey flinched. Yeah, she might have been jealous of Bridget because she'd wanted a chance to dance and chase her own dreams. But that didn't fit with Bridget; Bridget wasn't jealous of anyone.

When Lindsey looked up, Ms. Mulberry watched her with a worried expression. "Things aren't moving along as fast as I thought they were. Oh well." She shoved her chair back and groaned as she got to her feet. "It's time you got going. You have a lot to do." She came behind Lindsey, pulled her up out of the chair, and shoved her toward the door. "Go on. Life doesn't wait forever."

"Wait." Lindsey stumbled, trying to turn around, but Ms.

Mulberry's shove was relentless. "Stop. I don't know what I'm supposed to do."

Grabbing Lindsey by both shoulders, Ms. Mulberry brought her around and stared directly into her eyes. "Of course, you do. You get that witch and save your sister. The amulet you're wearing is all the help you'll need. When in doubt, use it however you can. Sling it, throw it, stomp on it if necessary. I don't know more than you when it comes to that, but you'll figure it out."

She started to force Lindsey back around but stopped and jerked her back. "Oh, and one more thing. The easiest way to defeat a witch is to use her own magic against her. Beat that batty with her own tricks." She winked and swung Lindsey around so fast Lindsey tripped over her own feet.

Before Lindsey caught her balance, she found herself back out on the landing with the door slammed shut behind her.

A *clunk-clunk-clunk* of three deadbolts was her only goodbye.

The hallway at the dance school stretched out darker than usual. The wooden floorboards creaked, and the brick walls appeared muddier than before. Lindsey clenched her hands at her sides as she made her way to the office and ignored the uneasiness building inside. She didn't have time to second-guess anything. She had to find Bridget.

Defeat the witch. Ms. Mulberry's words didn't bring her calm. If anything, it made the whole task seem even more unimaginable.

When Lindsey reached the huge picture of Madame Destinée hanging on the wall, she stopped. The first day she'd seen it, she'd been impressed by the *grand jeté.* Now it made her cringe. There was nothing beautiful about Madame Destinée. Even the smile she had found bright before was a sneer.

But that was fine. Let the picture glare and sneer. Lindsey had no intention of playing nice anymore. She'd come to get Bridget back. No matter what.

Something smashed against her leg, nearly bowling her over.

"Broussard!" She dropped to her knees and scratched him. He nudged his nose against her leg. "You scared me." His fur was warm and comforting.

After a scratch or two, he pulled away and scurried down the hall. About midway, he stopped, peered back at her, and whined as if he were trying to say something.

"Is she here?" Lindsey whispered. All was still dark. The light didn't shine behind the office door, which had to be a good sign.

Broussard padded to Madame Destinée's office and stopped right in front of it until Lindsey caught up to him. The door handle *clicked* as she pushed it down and peered inside.

A dim, bluish light gleamed from the other side of the office, and a low, mechanical moan of metal and gears rumbled and purred. Holding her breath, Lindsey pushed the door a little wider. Although the office appeared as it always did, there was a gigantic, gaping hole in the far brick wall. It was perfectly round, an entrance to another room.

Lindsey opened the door, but a movement made her jerk it partially closed again, so only her head could peek through.

"Isn't it lovely?"

Madame Destinée walked past the opening in the wall and swirled into the room beyond. She appeared to be talking to someone behind her, but Lindsey didn't see anyone. It was hard to discern anything against the eerie, bluish light, but she could make out a music box big enough for a life-sized figurine. It wasn't like the music boxes on Madame Destinée's shelves. The lid was missing, and a giant flower bud stood on the pedestal where the figurine would have been. The bud was beautiful. The petals were made of tulle, the same cloth used for a tutu. So soft and fluffy. They lapped over each other in gentle layers. Red, yellow, blue, and greens formed a kaleidoscope of colors.

Madame Destinée strode toward the music box, leaned over, and clutched a golden knob on the pedestal. She turned it as if to wind up the gigantic music box.

"What is it?" Adela appeared from behind the music box. She giggled as she walked around and stared at the colorful bud.

"It's a music box. My brother created it for me." Madame Destinée continued to crank.

"*La caja de música es bella.*"

"Yes, it is beautiful. When a talented ballerina enters the center of the bud, it blooms into a gorgeous flower. But only when the dancer is very talented. It won't work on everyone. Would you like to give it a try?"

"*Sí!*" Adela bounded up a small set of stairs on one side of the box and gazed at the sleeping flower. "What do I do?"

"Push through the cloth and go inside."

Adela gently shoved through the layered petals of tulle and

disappeared into the flower bud.

"*Es bella!* So soft. So many colors! And it glows...*las luciérnagas!*"

"Yes, I suppose it does glisten like fireflies." Done turning the knob, Madame Destinée stepped back through the hole in the wall into the office and continued to the water dispenser. She took a paper cup from a stack on the side, filled it with water, and returned to the giant sleeping bud.

"Are you ready, darling?"

"*Sí!*"

Reaching up onto her tiptoes, Madame Destinée emptied the cup over the top of the closed bud. The water soaked into the petals, and the bud shimmered and glowed. When Madame Destinée came back down the stairs, she hit a gold button next to the knob.

"Oi!" Adela's gasp came from inside the flower. "The floor is moving!"

"The music box will spin for you. All you must do is hold a beautiful dance pose."

The bud bloomed. Layer after layer, the soft petals swung outward and formed a gorgeous, twinkling flower. In the middle danced Adela. She *révèled en pointe* and performed one *pirouette* after another—so straight and high and graceful.

"I don't hear music. No *funciona?*" Stretching higher and higher, Adela's voice strained.

Madame Destinée shook her head. "No, it isn't broken. It's your posture. It's not quite right. Hold your chin high and relax those fingers. Imagine that you are the most graceful ballerina in the world."

Adela extended her arms and legs gracefully while the box made her turn.

It was beautiful—amazing. Lindsey poked her entire upper body through the opening in the door. She couldn't have looked away if she wanted to. The music box glowed as if caught in an enchanting, magical spell. Little flickers of light sprinkled the air around Adela as the flower opened completely. A ball of stars encased her.

With all of the glittering light, it appeared as if Adela was shrinking.

Lindsey rubbed her eyes, sure she wasn't seeing correctly, but when she looked again, Adela was already as tall as Broussard. With every spin, she became smaller and smaller. If it continued, there wouldn't be anything left of her!

Madame Destinée remained still with her arms crossed over her chest and watched. So cold. So cruel.

Lindsey dug her fingers into her palms. She had to say something to stop it. She couldn't let Adela die! But before she could burst into the office, Broussard snagged the back of her jean's leg and yanked her backward. She barely caught the doorframe in time to keep from landing on her backside.

"What are you doing?" she hissed between clenched teeth.

He scurried back a couple of steps and whined.

By the time Lindsey peered back into the office, Adela was nowhere to be seen. Madame Destinée strode over to the open flower and leaned over it. Carefully, she lifted a music box out of the middle. It was a red music box with golden bands around the edges. In the center stood a tiny figurine frozen in an eternal *pirouette*—Adela.

Lindsey gasped and slapped her hand over her mouth to block the noise.

Madame Destinée spun around and squinted to see into the shadows of the office. "Who's there? Broussard?"

Broussard tugged at Lindsey's leg, but she didn't have to be told. She turned and bolted down the hallway. Her heart thundered in her chest. Madame Destinée had turned Adela into a music box!

Her boots skid, and she stumbled twice. She couldn't fall. Not now. She had to leave the school before Madame Destinée noticed she'd been there.

At the door, she gripped the handle and yanked it open, but it rammed into something on the floor. The door was blocked. Lindsey glanced down to find Broussard sitting on his haunches.

"Broussard! Move!" She shoved him with the side of her foot, not wanting to hurt him, but she had to get out of there at any cost.

"I could have sworn I heard someone." Madame Destinée's voice echoed down the hallway.

"Come on," Lindsey grumbled and bent down to pick Broussard up out of the way.

"Oh darling, it's you."

Lindsey's legs gave way, and she fell to her knees on the floor. It was over. There was no way she could hide anymore. Madame Destinée had caught her.

Broussard jumped onto her lap and forced his way under her arms, but she barely noticed his presence. She had failed. She didn't save Bridget. She couldn't even save herself. Madame Destinée was going to shrink her now, too.

"Broussard! Oh, that silly dog." Madame Destinée's heels clicked sharply against the hallway floor.

Warm fur nuzzled against her chin, and a paw settled on her cheek. Lindsey peered down, meeting Broussard's gaze. His sweet doggy eyes told her she wasn't alone. She sucked in air and hugged him tighter, burying her face against his head. "Help me," she whispered. She'd never been so scared. Her whole body shook. Even the world blurred before her eyes.

"Did he jump on you again?" Madame Destinée blocked the light above, leaving Lindsey in a shadow. "I know you're always so excited to see her, Broussard, but you should at least let her come in through the door."

A wet lick against Lindsey's face and then Broussard bounded away. A whine pulled at her throat as cold and fear rushed in where his warmth had been before. She couldn't do this; she couldn't face Madame Destinée.

"Well, darling, I'm assuming you've come to practice. You are determined, but that shouldn't surprise me. I knew it the moment I saw you that you have everything it takes to make it in this business. Before you go to the studio, though, I want you to join me in my office. There's something I'd like to discuss with you."

Fingers wrapped around Lindsey's arm, guiding her to her feet. She didn't fight it. It wouldn't do any good. If she remained calm, she might be able to figure a way to escape. After all, Madame Destinée thought she'd just arrived. She didn't know she'd seen Adela and the gigantic music box.

Whatever calm Lindsey managed to gather shattered as they headed toward the office door. *The giant music box!* Madame Destinée was going to shrink her, too!

Nearing the door, terror hammered through her. Every part of her screamed to run, but she couldn't. Not if she wanted to find Bridget.

The office was as it'd always been during the days before. The hole in the wall was gone, along with the giant music box. It took everything Lindsey had not to sigh in relief.

"Last night's performance was amazing, darling. *You* were amazing." Madame Destinée moved behind her desk and motioned Lindsey to sit down. "I can't wait to see what your performance will hold tonight." She gave a genuine smile.

You need to catch a witch. Mulberry's words echoed in her head as Lindsey gazed at the desk. Two music boxes stood there. Madame Destinée lifted the red one with gold trimming and carried it to the shelf.

Adela. Lindsey's gut twisted.

The music box still standing on the desk was different than the rest. This one was polished brown wood with a few trims of gold here and there. It wasn't as fancy as the others, but it appeared to be more precious than the rest of the boxes.

Something about it reminded Lindsey of her dream. *"Stretch higher, darling."* A shiver ran through her as she remembered her toes glued to the pin. Just like Adela's. Lindsey stared at the box, wanting to look away. But she couldn't.

"Now, darling, do tell me what's wrong. You're as white as snow."

"Nothing," Lindsey squeaked and hugged her arms around her stomach. She had to stay calm and normal. Madame Destinée wasn't allowed to suspect a thing.

Madame Destinée rambled on about something...Lindsey had no clue about what. She didn't hear a single word above the noise of her own thoughts. Hundreds of dancers were trapped on the wall next to her. She could feel them. Every single one. It made her want to cry.

"Lindsey?" Madame Destinée leaned over the desk, tapping at the wood with her fingernails. "What are you thinking, child?"

She pressed her fingers into her legs. "Nothing."

"That is not the impression I'm getting." Madame Destinée rose from her chair and came around the desk directly in front of Lindsey. "Most dancers would be thrilled after giving a performance such as yours. They'd never pull such a sad face as I see now. It's no use lying to me, so you might as well tell the truth. What's bothering you?"

Lindsey balled her fingers. She could do this. For Bridget. "My little sister Bridget disappeared last night. You haven't seen her, have you?" She spoke fast. Way too fast.

"Oh, darling! That's awful. I'm so sorry for you. I wish I could help, but I can't even recall you ever mentioning that you had a sister."

All fear focused into a glare, one Lindsey barely held back. *Liar*. She'd mentioned her sister. Madame Destinée herself had asked about her.

"Is there anything I can do to help?"

Anger burned, but there was no way she could let Madame Destinée see it. Locking her gaze on her fingers, Lindsey tried to think fast. "I'd like to have Bridget's ticket for the show tonight. You asked me to bring her with me, so she could watch me dance."

"Is that so? Hmm, now that you mention it, I do remember something like that. But do you expect to find her by tonight?"

"I'll find her." Lindsey swore she would.

"If you don't know where she is, how can you be sure? Children go missing all the time, especially in large cities like New York. I'm not implying that it's all right. It isn't. But life is full of dangers."

The uncaring attitude in Madame Destinée's voice made Lindsey finally glare up, but Madame Destinée had turned away to stare at the boxes. She licked her lips—Ellie, Adela, Sanae Aito, and Robert. Desire dripped off her every move.

Fighting back the queasiness inside, Lindsey wrapped her

arms tighter against her stomach.

"So, can I have it?" she blurted out, unable to bear sitting there any longer.

Madame Destinée sighed and flicked her wrist as if the thought was a pesky gnat. "I'll make sure they know at the door. If you find her, tell her to go to the entrance on the other side of the building. I'm sure she'll find it."

The other side. Lindsey shook her head. She hadn't realized it before. They were in New York; there was an alleyway on the other side of the building. The garbage truck had backed up halfway into it the first time she'd met Madame Destinée. But it was stinky and trashy, not the way people would want to walk to enter a theatre.

Then, it hit her. There wasn't another entrance to the theatre. There had never been an audience. That's why the chairs were empty.

Everything was a lie.

Madame Destinée didn't peer over when Lindsey stood to leave. Her gaze moved down the row of music boxes. Her lips whispered as she passed each one—she was counting them.

Lindsey wondered why. It couldn't be a good thing. It gave her the creeps.

As soon as she went through the door, she bolted down the hallway. As before, Broussard bounced in front of her as soon as she reached the door and blocked it with his fuzzy backside.

"Aw, come on, Broussard. Move it." She was in no mood to mess with this again. Peering back to make sure Madame Destinée wasn't following, she leaned down and picked him up. As she lifted him, something dropped out of his mouth.

Clinkity-clank-clank. A set of keys hit the floor.

"Those are Mom's!" She dropped to her knees, set Broussard down, and picked them up.

Clinkity-clank-clank.

She froze. It was the same noise she'd heard the night before on the stairwell, when she'd snuck out of the apartment building. The memory of the eyes in the dark played through her mind. A person had chased her…followed her. She gasped as realization hit.

Bridget. It had been Bridget who followed her. She was there in the school. Somewhere. She had to be.

Ruf. Ruf. Broussard bounced away, leaving the door free.

But Lindsey couldn't go, not knowing Bridget was close.

"Broussard, stop that! I don't know what's gotten into you lately." Madame Destinée huffed from behind as Broussard's paws clicked into overdrive.

Lindsey sucked air. As long as Madame Destinée was around, she couldn't do anything. She'd have to sneak in later and look when Madame Destinée wasn't paying attention.

Stuffing the keys into her pocket, Lindsey got to her feet and grabbed the door handle. "Don't worry, Bridget. I'll be back. I'll find you and bring you home," she whispered and walked out the door.

The second she returned home, Lindsey leaned against the wall in the hallway and lowered to the floor. Tears coursed down her cheeks. She could barely breathe. It was all too much, way too much. She wanted to be brave, but she wasn't. Not even a little.

The memory of Adela shrinking played through her mind again and again. And then there was Bridget. She pictured her to be trapped in a cold, dark room with nothing but a wet, hard floor to sit on. Madame Destinée was evil.

Robert, Ellie, Sanae Aito...every one of them was trapped, turned into figurines.

It was unimaginable, but it was true. Lindsey had seen it herself.

She pushed her face down against her legs. She didn't know what to do. There was nothing she could do. Madame Destinée was a real witch with magic and spells. How was she supposed to go up against someone like that?

It was hopeless. Even if she found Bridget, Madame Destinée wouldn't let her walk out of the dance school with her. She'd try to stop her. She might even come to the apartment. Madame Destinée had already delivered the cakes and made Mom and Dad forget Bridget's existence. Ms. Mulberry was wrong. She could never defeat a witch.

"Lindsey."

Tears dripped from her nose and chin, but she didn't bother to wipe them away. It didn't matter. Nothing did.

"Lindsey."

Pushing her hair out of her face, she sat back up and stared at her bedroom door. A voice buzzed in her head, calling out to her.

"Lindsey!" The small voice sounded urgent.

"The music box!" Her boots squeaked as she scrambled over the floor, into her room, and crashed down onto the sleeping bag.

The ballerina stood on the pedestal in the middle of the box and blinked up. Lindsey grasped the box and brought it to eye level. "Do you know how to stop her? Do you know how to save Bridget?"

"You must save them all."

"But how? How can I save them all?"

"The charm that guards against jealousy."

"My amulet?" She jammed her hand down her shirt and pulled it out. Ms. Mulberry had said it was the key to everything. "So, you know how it works?"

"It will help protect you, but the real strength will come from within."

Lindsey clutched the charm in her palm, wishing that made sense. "What about Bridget?"

"Madame Destinée will use Bridget soon. Whenever the music plays, she steals our talent."

"You mean, whenever the music boxes play? Is that how it works?" It was inconceivable, but so was magic and tingly food and Adela shrinking into a music box. Lindsey slumped down and stared at the amulet. The figurine said it would help but offered fewer details than Ms. Mulberry. "I don't know how to stop her. I can't."

"I was the first one to be drained, a long time ago. The Madame didn't know how it worked, not completely. First, she drained my talent. Then, she drained my life. All that's left is my soul."

Lindsey wrapped her arms around herself to fight away

growing coldness although the room was warm. "You're dead?"

"And still trapped. She placed me in a corner, leaving me to remain forgotten. That's why Madame didn't notice when I went missing, stolen by one of her students. On her way home, she was distracted by friends, set me down on a park bench and forgot me. Soon, I was taken again by an older woman and placed on a shelf in her shop. That's when your grandmother found me. She recognized the quality of my box."

"And you became my birthday present." It was a lot to digest, and the more Lindsey thought about it, the more nauseated she felt.

"You must stop her before she drains the rest. She uses the others but doesn't drain them completely. She only takes enough for her performances. The rest she is saving. For what, I don't know."

Robert, Ellie, Adela, Sanae Aito... All of them were stuck on pins, waiting to dance—waiting for Madame Destinée to steal their talent.

And Bridget.

Lindsey wrapped her fingers around the amulet until her hand grew damp from sweat. She didn't know how she was going to pull this off, but she had to save them. She was the only one who knew what Madame Destinée was trying to do.

"Okay. Fine." She closed her eyes, praying she was braver than she felt. "What do I need to do?"

*L*indsey pushed her head back into her pillow and stared at the night sky through the bedroom window. The figurine in her music box had told her to find a button and open the wall to the hidden room. There she'd find the machine. With the machine, Lindsey could change the music boxes back into dancers.

Or something like that.

With a huff, she flopped over and picked at the edge of her pillowcase. The figurine hadn't given many details. The poor wooden dancer didn't seem to know too much more than what she'd witnessed herself, which wasn't much.

She desires your talent most of all. The music box had repeated those words several times.

If Lindsey wasn't careful, she'd end up a music box herself.

Shoving the thought into the far corners of her mind, Lindsey crawled out of her sleeping bag and picked up the music box. Although the ballerina inside said it was too late for her to be rescued, Lindsey couldn't leave her like this. She'd once been a real girl, too.

The thought weighed her down, but she held the feeling back behind an invisible wall. Tonight, she had to be brave.

After placing the metal, sleep-inducing box onto the floor of her parent's bedroom, Lindsey snatched her coat and stuffed the music box with the poor ballerina inside by her stomach. She zipped the coat shut. The bulge made her appear super fat, but it'd have to do because it'd never fit in her pocket.

"You can do this." Holding onto those words, she left the apartment.

She hoped she'd get to see it again.

At Ms. Mulberry's door, she put up her hand to knock but

stopped. On the floor lay a paper rose with a tiny note taped to it. Bending down, she picked it up.

Love is the most powerful magic of all.

Lindsey hiccupped a sniff. If love was all she needed, freeing Bridget would be easy. Too bad it probably wouldn't work that way. For some reason though, the thought helped. Stuffing the note into her pocket, Lindsey continued down the stairs and out the door.

A misty cloud covered the street, and everything was still. Lindsey jogged down the sidewalk, around the corner, and down the other side of the block. The light from the dance school reflecting against the icy sidewalk broke through the darkness. She skidded to a stop in front of the door and pushed down on the door handle. It moved stiffer than usual and didn't want to click. She pushed again.

The door was locked.

"Hello?" If she didn't get in, she couldn't save Bridget. "Is anybody there? I'm here for the show! Open the door, please!" She pushed at the handle again and again, but it didn't budge.

Lindsey shoved her nose against the glass on the door, trying to peer inside. Everything was dark. That didn't make sense. The show was about to begin. Madame Destinée wanted her to perform; she was supposed to dance a solo. Plus, if Madame Destinée locked her out, she'd never be able to capture her. She'd never be able to steal her talent.

Lindsey would never be able to save Bridget.

"Let me in! Please, let me in!" The glass rattled under the onslaught of her fists. Madame Destinée had to let her inside. She just had to.

No one came.

The door pressed against Lindsey's back as she slid down onto the doorstep and dropped her head between her knees. This couldn't be happening. She had to save Bridget. She was ready to save her.

The night air lingered with a chilling caress and iced Lindsey's cheeks. She couldn't lose Bridget. There's no way she could live without her. She'd do anything to get her back!

"Please." Her sob echoed with the icy wind.

Click. The door moved behind her. Gulping air, she scrambled around to find a pair of beady eyes peering around the small crack as it opened.

"Broussard!" Her arms wrapped around his warm, furry body. "You've come to get me." She had no idea how he'd opened that door, but it didn't matter.

Ruf. Fighting his way free, he took off into the school, glancing back once as if to make sure she followed.

The hallway was empty and dark, but the soft, rhythmic thuds of dancers' feet echoed in the distance.

Click-click-click-click. Broussard's paws tapped against the wooden floor as he hurried to Madame Destinée's closed office door. When he reached it, he plopped down onto his haunches. His tongue hung out of his mouth, and he panted. Waiting.

Lindsey came up and scratched his head. "You're right. It's now or never."

With Madame Destinée gone, she had time to figure out how to open the hole in the wall. She hoped she'd be able to find out how the machine worked. Wrapping her fingers around the cold handle, she opened the office door.

Inside, everything sat dark. Too dark. She couldn't see a thing. Although Madame Destinée probably watched the show upstairs in the theatre, it'd be better not to take any chances and turn on a light. Luckily, the office didn't have much in it to begin with.

To open the passage to the other room, you must push the button by the spi-Gachoo! The figurine had sneezed the last part of the instructions, which wasn't exactly helpful. Neither was finding a button in the dark. Stretching her arms out in front of her, Lindsey shuffled forward. It was like playing Marco Polo in the swimming pool, but no one was there to answer her call with "Polo."

BLOOP. BLOOP.

"We know where the water dispenser is," she mumbled before ramming her shin hard into the chair behind Madame Destinée's desk. "Ouch. And here's the chair."

She rolled it back and plopped down onto the cushioned seat. The button was probably hidden in a drawer or under the desk, she decided. That's where buttons were always hidden in the movies.

BLOOP. BLOOP.

The drawer squeaked as she pulled it open. Inside, all sorts of small objects rolled about. Pencils and pens slid beneath her fingers. There was a rubbery square that must have been an eraser and a container with curls of cold metal. "Paper clips," she sighed. The slick surface of paper filled the rest of the drawer. But nothing felt like a button.

Broussard wrenched on her pant leg, making the entire chair roll back.

"Broussard, what are you doing?"

He yanked harder, trying to pull her from the chair. She kicked her leg to shake him loose, but he wouldn't let go. When the chair knocked up against something, he finally stopped.

BLOOP. BLOOP.

She reached out her hands to feel the cool, smooth plastic bottle of the water dispenser.

"You're thirsty? We don't have time for that."

Then, it hit her. *Spigot.* The ballerina hadn't sneezed. She'd said spigot. A waterspout! It wasn't hard to find the small plastic faucet even in the dark. Above it sat two circular buttons, one on the left and one on the right. Taking a deep breath, she pushed the button on the left.

A glowing drop of water appeared at the end of the spout, no bigger than the tip of her pinky finger. It glistened with a beautiful sea blue. A tiny *plop* and it plummeted to the floor, but it didn't splash and disappear into the carpet; it bounced like a tiny rubber ball. *Boing. Boing.*

Lindsey lowered to her hands and knees and followed the drop until it reached the wall. With new gusto, it rolled straight up the bricks, higher and higher. Lindsey had to climb to her feet to keep the glowing drop in her line of sight. When the droplet was half-way up, it squished flat and began to spread.

It reminded Lindsey of a growing puddle during a rain as it

125

expanded across the wall's surface. Lindsey dabbed at it with her fingertip expecting the surface to be wet, but her finger passed through the water and right through the wall! The blue faded, leaving a perfectly round hole in the wall—the entrance. On the other side, brightly lit, was the room from before.

Broussard yipped and jumped right through the opening. On the other side, he turned a circle, panting with excitement. All around him, on the floor, stacked on shelves, and piled up on a big work bench along all three walls, were hundreds of toys. In the center stood the gigantic music box.

"Wow!" Lindsey went through, careful not to step on anything. Wind-up trains, monkeys with cymbals, dolls with joints, airplanes tied to the ceiling—all sorts of toys spread out in all directions, dusty and forgotten. On a nearby work bench, a painted metal horse lay on its side. Its last leg still needed to be screwed on. A brass knob like the one on the music boxes stuck out of its back. She picked it up and wound it. The three legs clattered up and down in a funny trot. Laying the horse back down, she turned to the giant music box.

Up close, it was even more beautiful. The closed bud rose into the air, proud and gentle at the same time. The surface sparkled, and little glimpses of light danced in and out in their own ballet. She reached up and poked one of the giant petals. It felt like her tutu, soft and spongy.

Broussard pawed her leg, stared at the office door, and whimpered.

"She's coming." Lindsey didn't have to speak dog to understand that.

Broussard bounded to the water dispenser and stared up at the spigot.

"Push it again. Got it."

She dashed over, pushed the button, and with a sudden *cur-splash*, the edges of the hole collapsed. The entire office went dark.

"Broussard? Where are you?" Madame Destinée's voice came from somewhere in the hallway.

Lindsey reached out until her fingers hit the desk and followed it around until she reached the chair on the other side. There was no place to hide, but if she sat in the chair and pretended to be sad she missed the show, Madame Destinée might believe her. It was a long shot, but she couldn't think of anything else. Panic made that impossible.

Madame Destinée's shoes clicked in the hallway, coming closer and closer.

Lindsey plopped down in the chair, forcing tears to her eyes. Not that it was hard. Fear pushed her to the verge of tears anyway. She leaned forward making herself as small as possible, but the music box inside her coat dug into her stomach. Oh no! Madame Destinée was sure to see it. Her fingers shook as she grabbed the zipper and opened her coat. Pulling out the music box, she bent forward to the floor and shoved it under the desk. She barely made it back into the chair before the door opened.

*L*ight flooded the office. Lindsey squished into a tight ball and closed her eyes. Tears flowed freely, and her entire body quivered and quaked. Coming into the office was a stupid idea. She was trapped. Again.

"Broussard, here you are."

Cloth rustled as Madame Destinée came into the room. Broussard whined. Something shifted, there was a knock, and then came a loud huff followed by the scrambling of paws over the carpeted floor. Lindsey tightened.

A slight breeze brushed against her cheek, carrying a faint hint of the stench from the backstage upstairs. When a cold, pointy finger poked under her chin, Lindsey's heart stop. She let her face be tilted upward but refused to open her eyes.

"Have you been sitting here this whole time alone, crying in the dark? But why? I was waiting for you. The audience was so excited to see you dance."

"I tried." Lindsey gulped for words. Her mind raced to think of an explanation. "The front door was locked. I couldn't get in."

"It was locked?" The finger pulled away. "Did you push down hard enough? It is cold in New York. It might have frozen a bit. I never lock it. Why would I..."

There was a yelp and then the scurrying of paws around the desk to the other side of the room. Nothing else moved for a moment. A long moment. Finally, Lindsey opened her eyes.

Madame Destinée stood over her, watching, but her expression remained calm and relaxed.

"See? Everything's fine, darling. There's nothing to cry about." With a sudden spin, she went to the other side of her desk. "I can only tell you how sorry I am that this evening's

128

performance didn't work out, but there's no need to worry or cry. Tomorrow's performance will be twice as grand."

Lindsey eased her legs to the floor as tears fell down her cheeks. If Madame Destinée expected her to dance in tomorrow's performance, she wouldn't be changing Lindsey into a music box quite yet. She still had a chance. Using the edge of her coat, she wiped the tears from her face.

Bloop. Bloop. Bloop. Lindsey snapped her head up. Madame Destinée stood at the water dispenser, filling a small cup. Nothing glowed. There wasn't a magical drop. Lindsey leaned closer to see Madame Destinée's finger sliding away from the second button, the one Lindsey hadn't pushed.

"Here, drink this. You'll need it considering the stress you've suffered today." Madame Destinée held the cup out to her over the desk.

While settling into the chair, Lindsey took it and stared down at the glistening surface. The water seemed to be normal.

"Go on, drink."

With the cup in her hands, Lindsey brought it to her lips. The water was cold and wet. Hoping that it appeared as though she was drinking it, she pretended to take a sip. She wasn't stupid enough to fall for any tricks again, not after the incident with Adela.

"The water is from France. That's one of the benefits of being able to be everywhere in the world and nowhere at the same time." Madame Destinée paused as if realizing she'd let that slip, but she quickly waved it off. "Oh, who am I fooling? I'm sure you and the others noticed my brother's clever invention right away—a type of transportation machine that allows the school to sit outside of normal time and space. The portals appear as doors to buildings, fitting right in wherever they're needed."

She tilted her head, eyeing Broussard's tail peeking from behind the water dispenser. "But he can't take all the credit. I added a talent of my own: magic."

Lindsey choked and spat into the cup. "Magic?"

"Surprised?" A beaming smile radiated from her face. "Scientists and fools might insist otherwise, but it does exist. Every culture from the beginning of time holds stories of witches and spells. It's ludicrous to believe that every single one comes from a silly fantasy. The similarities between the tales are impossible to deny. Plus, I'm living proof that the fools are wrong."

"You're a witch." Lindsey slapped her hand over her mouth, wanting to kick herself. Why couldn't she keep her mouth shut?

"Don't worry. The word isn't offensive. Quite the contrary. I had the fortune of running into a true master years ago. Such a darling. She used her talents to enhance costumes and props. The audience loved it, but what a shameful waste. Her talents could've allowed for much greater things. I've always treasured her cake recipe, though."

Ms. Mulberry? Wow! She *was* a witch, too. Ms. Mulberry had more than hinted at it, but hearing the word outright was completely different. Lindsey stuffed her hand into her pocket and clutched the paper flower, but she didn't pull it out. Just holding it gave her courage. Ms. Mulberry was a witch, and she believed Lindsey could defeat Madame Destinée. Maybe Ms. Mulberry was right.

"Unfortunately, my brother wasn't talented in the mystical arts. His attempts turned out rather badly." Again, she stared down at Broussard's tail.

Lindsey blinked as the truth hit her. Her mouth dropped open. She tried to say something, but her tongue refused to work.

"Oh, yes, darling. You've guessed it."

Whoa! Lindsey's brain flip-flopped. Broussard was Jeannot Broussard! She leaned forward, trying to see more than the tail. It was so weird to think the dog was really a man.

Madame Destinée slid the photograph of Jeannot toward her from across the desk. It was a man, definitely not a dog. But when she peered down to where Broussard hid again, he turned around and looked up at her. She glanced at the picture, and then stared at Broussard. There was a resemblance. Well, in a dog sort of way. She leaned back into the chair, with her head buzzing on overdrive. Witches and spells existed. Broussard was actually a man. There were machines that led outside of time and space and—

"You're pale, darling, but I suppose knowing Broussard is actually a man might cause that reaction. I have something which might take your mind off of that." Madame Destinée leaned over and opened a drawer. When she stood, a sparkling blue bundle rested in her arms. "I have another surprise for you." With a flick of her wrists, the cloth cascaded open.

Lindsey gasped. It was Madame Destinée's dress, the same one she'd worn in the picture in the hallway.

"This is for you." Madame Destinée carried it around the desk, holding it out.

"For me?" There was no way she would take it. Everything about the gesture screamed wrong.

"You are exceptional, Lindsey. You deserve to wear this costume. You are the dancer I've been waiting to find for years."

She swung it out for Lindsey to take it, but Lindsey cringed away. She wasn't going to touch that thing!

"Try it on. I insist." This time, Madame Destinée shoved it into her arms. Lindsey had no choice but to hold it. If she let it fall to the floor, it'd make Madame Destinée angry, and even though she knew nothing about witches, Lindsey didn't want an angry witch.

With a big swallow, she nodded and folded her arms around the soft cloth. She'd rather die than wear it, but if she didn't, she might die anyway. That thought made her swallow again.

"Go on, darling. I can't wait to see how it looks on you."

Digging her fingers into the cloth, Lindsey stood and headed toward the door. At least it'd get her out of the office and away from Madame Destinée for a while. Once in the dressing room, she'd have time to think. Maybe she'd find a way to get out of this mess and sneak off to search for Bridget.

As Lindsey walked through the office, Madame Destinée's stare weighed her down. Each step became a heavy task. Without thinking, Lindsey glanced up at the music boxes on the shelves. Adela's, Robert's, and Ellie's boxes stood silent and closed. Still, their cries for help hung unspoken in the air and in her heart. She wanted to help them, not just her friends but every single one. There were so many—three hundred and nineteen according to

Madame Destinée.

That was before Adela, Ellie, Sanae Aito, and Robert had been changed into music boxes. Adding them to the count made three hundred and twenty-three.

Three hundred and twenty-four.

Holding the number in her mind, Lindsey reached the office door. The poster Madame Destinée had taped up the day before now faced her—*Dancing in the Dawn of a New Year.*

Ellie had said that the theatre had three hundred and twenty-four seats.

Three hundred and twenty-three. The music boxes were one short of filling the theatre.

Lindsey froze.

One more music box and the seats would be full.

One.

She desires your talent most of all.

Lindsey's breath stuck. The last one was her! *She* was the missing figurine!

A metallic click snapped Lindsey out of her thoughts. Madame Destinée pulled her fingers back from the door handle. In her hand, she held a key.

"There's a different dressing room I'd like you to use, darling." She sauntered around the desk to the water dispenser and pushed a button.

A glowing droplet appeared.

Lindsey's feet rooted in place as the drop rolled over the carpet and onto the wall. The room opened up on the other side.

She grabbed the door handle and forced it down. It didn't budge. *No...no...no!* Her legs ached to run, but with the door locked, there was nowhere to go. With quivering fingers, she reached up and grabbed the amulet. Ms. Mulberry said it would help. Lindsey prayed it was true.

Holding the amulet tight, she turned to face the witch.

"So, darling, what do you think of my surprise?" Madame Destinée stepped up to the life-sized music box. Pride beamed from her.

Lindsey felt sick. She didn't respond or move. Her feet stuck to the floor. She wanted to get out of there, but it was useless. There was no escape.

Madame Destinée's expression fell, as if Lindsey's reaction wasn't what she'd hoped. "Tastes vary, I suppose. I've always found it to be Jeannot's most beautiful creation."

She rubbed her fingers over the soft, tulle bud, and Lindsey realized Madame Destinée expected her to gush over the flower as Adela had.

"It is gorgeous." Her voice was almost convincing…until she choked.

Madame Destinée continued to stroke the petals; they quivered under her touch. "The flower is a type of changing room. I thought you'd be honored to change into the dress inside of it, especially since you seem to appreciate Jeannot's work."

Lindsey nodded slightly, but the rest of her didn't budge. She'd never go near that terrible machine. Not in a million years. Madame Destinée would have to physically drag her over there, and if she did, Lindsey would bite, scratch, and kick the whole way.

"Fine, darling. You are making this difficult." With an exasperated sigh, Madame Destinée lifted something from the base of the giant bud. "I know you love these." Lindsey's pointe shoes dangled from her hand. "They are your favorite color and make your steps so lovely when you dance."

Back and forth, they swung.

Back and forth.

A light fog snuggled in at the back of Lindsey's mind, calm and comforting. Her thoughts muddled as they drifted into more soothing realms. How pretty the shoes were as they swung back and forth. She liked them more than any other shoes she'd owned before.

"Come, darling."

Lindsey moved. Her feet stepped softly over the carpet. Fog hung around her in a dream land. She loved dreaming. It was always nice and sweet.

Unless it was a nightmare.

A sudden stab inside her head made her flinch. *The witch.* There was a witch. A mean one. Or had she dreamt that? She wasn't sure.

The pointe shoes swung in a smooth rhythm. Constant. Never ending. How she loved to watch them!

"Go on, darling. Go up the stairs and step inside the bud."

The stairs slipped by as if they weren't even there. A wall of puffy cloth blocked her way. She poked at it. It bounced like a fluffy tutu. Giggling, she poked it again.

"Go on inside." The order was as sweet as an invitation to a waltz. She happily danced into the bud, pushing the layers of cloth aside.

"Wow." A cave of rainbows and fireflies surrounded her. She could have stared at the lights for days.

"Lovely, isn't it?"

Lovely? It was amazing! She stood among fairies and stars!

"Now, get dressed and don't forget these."

The pointe shoes clunked as they hit the floor next to her feet, and when they did, the world snapped. Lindsey blinked at the sparkly walls around her. She was inside the gigantic bud— she was trapped!

"Let me out!" She dug her fingers into the cloth, but it didn't part or give way. The layers molded together to form a solid wall of fluff. "Let me out!" She slammed her fists into the cloth, but her hands sank in a few inches with no effect. Kicking was useless, too. She dug her fingernails in deep and tried to rip it apart, but it did no good. She was stuck.

"Let me out of here!" She screamed again and again. Her voice became hoarse. There had to be a way out. It was only cloth. But every unsuccessful kick and punch left her more exhausted than before. Finally, she collapsed to the floor. Sweat and tears dripped down her face as she gulped for air.

"Are you done with the dramatics?"

Lindsey dropped her head between her knees, drained and weak. But no, she wasn't done. She'd never be done with it until the witch let her out.

"If you'd drank the water I gave you, you wouldn't suffer claustrophobia. Happiness cures so many problems."

And makes people easy to control. So, she'd been right about the water. It hadn't been as normal as Madame Destinée implied. Not that Lindsey was surprised. She'd never trust a witch.

Reaching up, she dug the amulet out from underneath her coat and shirt. It was warm from her body heat, or was it more than that? Ms. Mulberry had said it would protect her. Lindsey stared at the blue eye, wondering what she had to do.

Throw it, stomp on it...

Ms. Mulberry's words rang silly now. Useless.

She rubbed the smooth surface between her fingers. "Think. Think. Think," she whispered in her own wishful spell.

Madame Destinée still didn't realize Lindsey knew what this machine could do. The witch thought she was afraid of tight spaces.

It wasn't much, but it had to help.

Lindsey kneaded the amulet harder, wishing it'd speak to her as her music box had.

"Wonderful. I see you've regained control over yourself. Now, would you mind putting on the dress and shoes? I'd still love to see you in them."

Lindsey gazed down at the dress, now rumpled on the floor near her feet, and continued to rub the amulet. "How do you work?" she asked it. She knew it couldn't answer but wished it'd give her some clue. It didn't. Of course not. Frustrated, she jerked it up over her head, but it stuck on something and refused to come off.

Looking down, she noticed that the string jammed in her coat zipper. Tugging hard, Lindsey broke it free, and when she did, a plan spun in her head. It wasn't the greatest plan and probably counted more as a ridiculous long shot, but it was better than what she had so far, which was nothing.

Trying not to think of Madame Destinée's picture in the hallway, Lindsey changed into the dress. She reached back for the zipper, grabbed the amulet's string, and held it tight against the metal teeth. With a hard yank, the zipper zoomed up and jerked when it hit the string. She forced the zipper up again, tugging it to the point she was afraid it'd rip. But it worked. The zipper and string caught.

"Uh, Madame Destinée?" Her voice shook.

"Yes, darling?"

"I need some help. The zipper...it's stuck. I can't get the dress on."

The click of heeled shoes came closer from the other side of the petals. "Are you sure? Try again."

Lindsey grunted and groaned, pretending to try her best. "I can't. It won't move."

An annoyed sigh sounded so thick Lindsey could feel it. "Fine. Come out. I'll take a look."

Keeping courage close, Lindsey pushed her hands into the cloth petals. The layers parted, allowing her to pass. Madame Destinée waited on the other side. Her expression was anything but cheerful.

"Turn around, darling."

Lindsey spun down and around the stairs, making sure Madame Destinée remained on the steps between her and the giant bud. Ms. Mulberry had said the best way to defeat a witch was to use her own magic against her. If she could force Madame Destinée closer to the bud, she might be able to push her inside it and trap her there. That was the basic plan, anyway. Several details—like sealing the petals before Madame Destinée could get out—were still open, but Lindsey hoped those would somehow work themselves out. She opened and closed her sweating hands, reminding herself to stay brave as Madame Destinée's fingers dusted across the back of her neck.

"What on Earth is this?"

The amulet rammed hard against Lindsey's throat when Madame Destinée tugged the cord. The more she fumbled to get it free, the closer Lindsey backed into her, making her move back up the stairs to gain more space. "Stand still, darling. I almost have it free. There!"

The amulet dangled from Madame Destinée's fingers as she held it over Lindsey's shoulder to show her. Then, she wrapped it up in her fist and tossed it to the floor. Lindsey dove forward, but Madame Destinée caught her shoulders and held her in place.

"No one needs such a ludicrous trinket. Now, turn around and let me see you."

Lindsey bit down on her lip, forcing herself to ignore the amulet. She didn't need it for what she was about to do anyway.

"Go ahead, darling. Do a quick spin."

Lindsey turned to find Madame Destinée backing up the stairs to stand in front of the bud, giving Lindsey more space. It was better than Lindsey had planned. Stretching her arms over her head, she performed a simple *pirouette*.

"Lovely. The dress is perfect!" Madame Destinée clapped. Her face beamed.

Lindsey spun again. This time, she leaped up to the next stair and let the pirouette gain speed.

"That's wonderful! Marvelous!"

Keeping the momentum, Lindsey spun and spun, edging toward Madame Destinée with each turn. Tiny step by tiny step, Madame Destinée neared the bud.

A little bit more...

The moment Lindsey had her in the right spot, Madame Destinée reached out and grabbed her shoulders. Lindsey jerked to a halt.

"That's enough, darling."

The heels of Madame Destinée dark blue shoes rubbed against the bottom of the bud. She was so close! Lindsey moved closer, ready for the moment to bound forward and knock the witch into the bud, but when she bent her knees, Madame Destinée managed to tug Lindsey around to the side.

"Careful, darling! We don't want you to fall."

Madame Destinée held tight, refusing to let go. Face to face, Lindsey stared at the witch across from her. Their shoulders rubbed against the petals. Neither stood closer or farther from the flower.

The perfect moment had passed.

Lindsey's shoulders slumped as the witch's boney fingers dug into her skin.

"The dress is fantastic, as lovely as I'd hoped it'd be. I have a special surprise for you, one which you're sure to love. Go back inside the bud and turn your *pirouettes* again. If you do, the bud will open up around you into a beautiful flower." Continuing to hold Lindsey with one hand, she pushed between the layers of petals with the other.

No...no...

The inside of the bud appeared through the opening, and Lindsey's legs grew weak. There was no way she could go back inside. If she did, she'd never come out again. She'd become a music box figurine. She wanted to cry, run away, and scream. But it wouldn't help.

"Go inside, darling. I promise it's an experience you'll never forget."

Lindsey held back as Madame Destinée pulled the petals further apart, making room for her to step inside. Her heart pounded in her ears, and the world blurred into a buzz around her. She couldn't think. Couldn't move.

"Come, darling. A few steps."

Lindsey tried to pull away. Her knees shook so much she could barely stand. "No, I can't. I...I..."

A ball of gray shot up onto the music box and moved close to Madame Destinée's feet.

"Broussard, what are you doing now?" Madame Destinée released Lindsey and bent down to shoo him away.

It was the perfect chance.

With a grunt, Lindsey slammed into Madame Destinée's

back.

The witch stumbled and grabbed at the petals to steady herself, but Broussard bounded hard against her ankles. With a gasp, Madame Destinée tumbled head-first through the petals and landed with a crash. The cloth closed around the witch, swallowing her up.

Remembering how Madame Destinée had used the golden button before, Lindsey leapt to the floor and slammed her fist against it. The bud's gigantic petals quivered.

"Broussard!" The witch's scream curdled. "Let me out! Now!" The moans and bangs made it clear that she was trying to get out.

It'd worked! With a quick fist bump to the air, Lindsey grabbed the wind-up knob and turned it like Madame Destinée had done with Adela. Her sweaty hands slid across the metal as she twisted the knob again and again. She didn't think of stopping, afraid the witch might find a way to escape. Her arms ached, so much so that she was sure they might fall off. Finally, the knob refused to turn any more.

Madame Destinée's screams stopped. The bud held perfectly still, and then eerie laughter came from inside it.

"You think trapping me here will help you? You, foolish child. You see, darling, you need my help if you ever want to see your sister again. I'm the only one who can bring her back. Unless you like having her as your own personal music box."

Lindsey stumbled back a step. "You turned Bridget into a music box?" Bridget wasn't a dancer. She played the violin. Madame Destinée had to be lying because a violinist like Bridget had no idea how to spin a *pirouette*.

"Her talent is even greater than yours. Her feeling for the music and rhythm is genius. A dancer who possesses these talents will be unlike any to have ever danced on the stage. Such a dancer would be more than a star. I will be unforgettable."

Lindsey peered over at opening of the room and back into the office beyond where the music boxes lined shelf after shelf on the wall. One of them held Bridget.

Bridget.

Lindsey's legs gave way as her heart uttered a silent, desperate scream. She crumpled to the floor. Poor Bridget. This was all Lindsey's fault. She should have never told Bridget about the dance school; Bridget would have never followed her. She wouldn't have been caught and turned into a music box figurine.

"I'm ready to make you a deal, one I'm sure you won't refuse."

Pain cut through Lindsey's lip as she bit down on it, fighting back tears. She'd never make a deal with the witch, no matter what it was. She'd turned Bridget into a wooden figurine.

Getting to her feet, Lindsey went through the hole, back into the office, and headed to the water dispenser. Taking the cup Madame Destinée had given her earlier off the desk, she dumped the contents onto the floor. Then, she went to the water dispenser and filled it with the magical water. She assumed this was the water Madame Destinée had poured over the bud before. The water splashed over the edge and onto her hand as she carried it to the giant music box.

"Darling, aren't you listening? I said I'm willing to let your sister go."

Stretching up onto her toes, Lindsey dumped the water over the top of the flower. As with Adela, it soaked into the petals, making them sparkle and glow.

"What are you doing?" Madame Destinée's voice rattled the air. "No! You fool! You'll never figure out how to free her if you change me into a music box."

$\mathcal{L}$indsey gripped the empty cup in her fingers so tight her knuckles hurt. Everything Madame Destinée said was a lie. She'd free Bridget without her. It was Broussard's machine, after all. He had to know how it functioned.

"If you change me into a figurine not only will you lose Bridget, but my magic will disappear. It's my magic which has enabled you to dance as you've never danced before. Without it, you'll be nothing. Your talent will be worthless. You'll never dance again."

"That's not true!" Lindsey screamed.

The witch's magic had nothing to do with her ability to dance. As long as Lindsey wasn't turned into a music box, the talent was her own.

The witch lied. She was sure of it. Clinging to that thought as she backed down the stairs, Lindsey watched the bud open. The layers peeled back one at a time until the beautiful flower blossomed in full bloom. Where Adela had posed as a beautiful center, now a haggard figure crouched on its knees. Madame Destinée's head hung low with her shoulders hunched. The music box spun her around and around, but she stayed a stone.

Suddenly, the witch's head snapped up. Her glare slashed with pitch-black eyes that held no color. Just black—empty and hollow.

Lindsey stumbled as panic took hold. This wasn't Madame Destinée. This was a real witch, the kind sketched in old fairy tale books. The kind found in nightmares.

Black smoke seeped around the witch. She rose to her feet. The darkness churned tight, cloaking her in its evil wisps. It twisted and turned. Her fingers commanding every move.

Lindsey swallowed hard. She was toast.

"Do you believe I can be so easily pushed aside?"

The witch's arm rose, and the darkness sprung with it. Her skirt flapped as if caught in a stormy wind, but the air remained eerily silent.

"I will have your talent. You cannot escape me!"

Lindsey backed away as the smoke rose higher, circling with fingers of its own. It curved and curled, soaring into the air.

"This is your last chance, free me or lose everything." Madame Destinée's screech filled the room, making the metal toys quiver and shake. "Your talent, your sister, even your friends. You'll lose them all. Without my magic, you're nothing. Everything you've learned—every *pirouette* and spin—will trickle away from your memory. You'll be nothing, never able to dance again. Even the untalented fools at the Community Center will laugh at you. In destroying me, you destroy yourself!"

You'll be the most famous dancer of all. Bridget's words pricked. Becoming a prima ballerina was all Lindsey had wanted. It was the only dream she ever had.

"You're lying!" Lindsey's words vibrated the air.

But inside, she felt empty and small. Without the magic, she'd no longer be able to perform a *Grand Jeté* or *Bourrée* with the same elegance she had the days before. She'd be stuck with Mr. Lagunov and his terrible Community Center. But then if she lost her talent, she'd never dance again anyway.

Refusing to let the witch see her cry, she wiped away the tears from her eyes.

The witch continued to scream, and her smoke swirled, but she shrank.

"You will regret this." Instead of the hate Lindsey expected, sorrow mirrored in the witch's eyes. They held promises and dreams—all those things Lindsey clung to and wanted to have.

"You will lose all." It was a whisper, one that gnawed. "I smelled you from half way around the world. So strong your talent is. Can you sit in an audience, unnoticed and forgotten, knowing what could have been while your sister relishes in fame? While she gains all those things that could have been yours?"

Lindsey shook her head, fighting back the pain. It would hurt. The witch wasn't wrong, but it'd be worth it. Bridget was worth it.

"You're right. I will miss it. But I'll sit in that audience and cheer louder than anyone else when Bridget's on the stage. When she becomes famous, I'll be her biggest fan and never once be jealous again. Because she's my sister. I love her. And that's what sisters do."

"Fool!" With a blood-curdling howl, the witch threw back her head. She shrieked and screamed as the smoke tangled in waves around her. But she shrank. With every turn, her power visually faded.

Finally, the music box stopped turning and silence held.

Slowly, Lindsey climbed up the stairs and peered into middle of the flower. A black music box stood inside. On the pedestal sat a crumpled-over hag in a black dress. She wasn't beautiful. She wasn't graceful. She was ugly.

Ruf. Broussard jumped into the flower. With his paw, he flipped the lid closed.

*L*indsey lifted the witch's music box out of the flower and carried it to the desk. After setting it down, she stared up at the shelves. So many stood there. Too many.

Three-hundred-and-twenty-three.

All needed to be freed. Too bad she had no idea how to change them back.

"Hey, Broussard, you're the one who made the machine. Tell me how to turn the music boxes back into the people they once were."

In the room behind her, on the other side of the hole, Broussard sighed.

Then, there was a rattle and the thunk of paws against the floor. When she turned, he climbed the stairs to the giant music box with the amulet dangling from his mouth. At the center of the flower, he let it drop.

The petals glowed, sending off a cloud of sparkles that rose and hung in the air like a light dust. He returned to her, sat back on his haunches, and gazed at the music boxes on the shelves. He turned his head and nodded at the plain wooden one still on the desk.

"You want me to start with that one?"

With a short nod, Broussard plopped onto his stomach right in front of Lindsey's toes. She leaned down and scratched him between the ears. "Can the machine turn you back, too? If it can, you should go first."

He stared up with sad eyes.

Lindsey's smile died. It didn't seem fair. He had created the giant music box, the portal machine, and possibly the earbuds, but still, if it hadn't been for him, she would have never defeated the witch. She would never be able to work his machine, either.

"Are you sure?" But she didn't need to hear his sigh to know the answer. It wouldn't work on him because he wasn't a music box.

Promising herself that she'd find a way to help him too someday, she turned toward the wooden box and picked it up. Although it wasn't as fancy as the others, it was more beautiful than the rest of the music boxes combined. She rubbed her finger over the lid, wanting to open it. But something stopped her.

Bridget.

A light but steady beat vibrated beneath Lindsey's fingers. Her sister's heartbeat. She knew it without a breath's thought. Bridget was inside, and she was alive. A tear cascaded down Lindsey's cheek as she leaned over and kissed the lid. "I'm sorry."

Wrapping her hands carefully around the box, she carried it to the giant flower bud and placed it in the center.

"Please, be okay." She rubbed her finger over the lid and slowly backed away.

The moment Lindsey stepped down the stairs, the glittery dust swirled. Pulling tight together like a sparkly tornado, it grew and grew until it suddenly stopped and drifted back into a peaceful cloud. In the middle of the flower stood Bridget with a violin cradled in her arms.

"Bridget!" Lindsey jumped up the stairs and grabbed her into a huge bear hug. She squeezed her and buried her face under Bridget's pigtail. When she let go, Bridget stood and stared at the room and hole.

"Where are we?"

"At the dance school."

Bridget cocked her head to the side. "This is the Community Center?"

Lindsey shook her head. "No, the other dance school. The one with the shows I had to sneak out for."

Bridget's face remained blank.

"You don't remember?"

Bridget shook her head.

Taking Bridget's arm, Lindsey guided her to Madame

Destinée's desk chair. She told her about the magical food and about how Bridget went missing. She didn't tell her that Mom and Dad had forgotten about her. That'd be too much, and she secretly hoped the spell on them had broken now that Madame Destinée was locked up in a music box.

"And that's what happened," she ended with a deep breath.

Bridget blinked with wide eyes, taking the story in without a single question. But she constantly peered over at the black music box on the desk with a look of distrust. "And you're sure the witch is stuck in there?"

Lindsey nodded. "Yep. She can never hurt anyone again."

"Are you super sure?" Bridget pushed the chair farther from the desk.

"Yeah. Why?"

Bridget lifted a shaking finger to point at the box. Her face paled. "Black smoke is coming out of it."

Lindsey grabbed Bridget's arm, jerked her out of the chair, and tugged her away from the desk as a long tentacle of black smoke stretched toward them. The lights in the office went out, and Bridget screamed. Everything went dark, except for the sparkling light from the flower in the room behind them. The beautiful light cast shadows, and it was in these dark places the lengthening limbs grabbed.

"You thought I was powerless because I shrunk?" The words chilled along with the air around them.

Lindsey shoved Bridget behind her, pushing her from the desk.

"You may be willing to give up your dreams to save your sister, but I'm not willing to give up mine. If you won't free me, I will destroy you. Not only will you never become famous, but you'll never see your sister in the spotlight, either."

A claw formed at the end of the smoky arm, and before Lindsey understood what was happening, it shot forward right toward her.

"No!" Bridget shoved Lindsey from behind, knocking her out of the way. She let out a horrible scream as the claw slammed into her chest and disappeared inside her, as if digging for her heart.

"Bridget!" Lindsey ran to pull her away, but the smoke thickened around Bridget, creating a dark cloudy shield. "Bridget!"

She had to do something...anything to save Bridget!

"Stop! You wanted me! Not her! Take me! Leave her alone! I'll give you my talent. All of it. Just let her go!"

A crackling laugh haunted the air. "A dancer or a violinist. Does it matter which talent I destroy? If you want me to stop, free me. Only then will this come to an end." The smoke thickened.

Bridget slumped forward.

"No!" Lindsey dove at the desk and grabbed Madame Destinée's music box.

The smoke oozed down, circling her fingers with frosty cold. It stung like a thousand needles, but even pain wouldn't make her let go.

"I love my sister! I'll never let you hurt her!"

Lifting it above her head, Lindsey slammed the box against the corner of the desk. The lid cracked. She slammed it again. And again. The wood split. The lid broke away. Splinters remained in her hands as the black smoke finally dissipated. Looking down, Lindsey saw the ugly figurine broken at the waist, its face caught in an eternal scream.

Letting the pieces fall to the floor, she raced back to Bridget and was engulfed in a tight hug

"You did it! You killed the witch."

Lindsey pulled her back and stared down at her chocolate-brown eyes. "Are you okay? You were screaming like crazy. It must have hurt."

"A little. Okay, a lot. But you stopped her. You smashed the witch to pieces." Bridget tugged on her pigtails. "I think we deserve a celebration doughnut. A pink one. With sprinkles." She paused for a moment before adding, "And not the tingly kind."

Lindsey nodded quickly. "Deal."

Although her body ached, and she wanted to go home and crawl into bed, Lindsey got to her feet and went to the shelves of music boxes. It was time to free the dancers, too. But first, she wanted to free the figurine in her own music box.

She crawled under the desk and carefully brought it out.

"That's yours! The one from Grandma," Bridget said.

"Yep. It was one of Madame Destinée's." She was about to tell Bridget the figurine had spoken to her but decided not to. Not yet. The whole thing was unbelievable enough as it was.

When she placed the box into the flower, the glistening cloud rose and spun. As it dissipated, there wasn't a girl but rather a bluish bubble about the size of a tennis ball. It glimmered and rose into the air. When it hit the ceiling, it disappeared.

Lindsey placed her hand on her chest as a happy feeling settled inside. *Thank you* whispered in her head.

"What happened? Wasn't there supposed to be a girl inside?"

"Not in that one." She didn't tell Bridget more than that and never would. Her ballerina had found peace.

Hoping that was the only drained music box, Lindsey turned toward the shelves. "Looks like we have a lot of work ahead of us."

One after another, she set the music boxes inside the flower. Like Bridget, none of the dancers remembered the dance school or Madame Destinée. Their eyes were blank as they sputtered out tons of questions—usually in languages she couldn't understand. At first, Lindsey didn't know if she could let them go like that. It didn't seem right. They deserved to know what had happened. But Broussard nodded his head to the door, signaling for her to show them the way out.

"And they'll end up back at home? Just like that?" Bridget asked as Lindsey reached for the next music box. "What if they've been missing for years?"

Lindsey paused, her fingers brushing the smooth sides of the painted wood on the next music box. "I don't know."

She had no clue how long Madame Destinée had been capturing dancers. Some of them could have gone missing a long time ago. If their families were still looking for them? Or had they forgotten about them like Mom and Dad forgot about Bridget? Lindsey chewed on her bottom lip as the weight of it settled in from all sides. She couldn't imagine how terrible it'd be to arrive back home only to find that her *home* was no longer there.

Arms encircled Lindsey's waist from behind, and Bridget squeezed hard. "No matter what happens, anything is better than letting them remain trapped here."

Turning around, Lindsey wrapped her arms around Bridget. The hug helped, and Bridget was right. If the dancers were left as wooden figurines, that would be worse. But still, some of those dancers would be thrown into another nightmare. It didn't seem fair.

A furry warmth shoved between Lindsey's and Bridget's legs. Broussard grunted as he joined the hug and stared up at them with knowing eyes...and something else.

"Broussard knows everything will be okay." Releasing Lindsey, Bridget bent down and scratched his head. "Will the dancers be okay, Broussard?"

He yelped and wagged his tail.

"See? And if anyone would know, it'd be him. After all, he's the one who built the machine, you said." A smile grew over Bridget's face, one that warmed like a dawning day.

Bending down, Lindsey joined Bridget and scratched his other ear. "Yes, he did."

She didn't know how the transporter worked, but it had brought the dancers to the practices and midnight shows at the same time everyday no matter where they lived in the world. If it could bend time enough for that, maybe it could do even more. Either way, she trusted Broussard.

After Lindsey led the first couple of dancers out the door, Bridget happily joined in to make things go faster. The hours stretched on, but not a single box could be left behind.

As Ellie appeared, Lindsey jumped up onto the flower and threw her arms around her. "I'm so glad you're back!" She hugged her hard, smashing her face into Ellie's black curls. They smelled sweet, like Grandma's honeysuckle bushes.

But Ellie stiffened. "Who are you?"

Lindsey stepped back. Her heart dropped like a stone. "You don't remember me?"

Ellie shook her head.

Of course, she didn't. Lindsey bit the inside of her cheek. Ellie would have made such a great friend, but being from Sweden, she'd probably never see her again anyway. It didn't seem fair or right.

"Here, I'll show you how to get home." Not letting disappointment show, Lindsey took her hand and led her to the door. Ellie continued out into the hallway without a single word or parting glance. The door closed behind her with a dead thud.

When Lindsey looked back, only two boxes remained: Adela and Robert.

Lindsey placed Adela's music box inside the flower and waited until she stood there in life-size. Her glare beamed as fierce as her red dress. She didn't say anything as Bridget went up and led her to the door, though. Like the others, she didn't remember anything. Lindsey wished she could. If anyone needed to learn from the experience, it was her. But all Lindsey could do was send her on her way and wonder why Adela continued to glare like she hated the world.

When Lindsey carried the last box to the machine, she paused and closed her eyes to make a quick wish. This one belonged to Robert. If anyone would remember what had happened, it had to be him.

She watched as the magic spun in the flower and Robert grew back to his original size. She held her breath as he blinked and gazed around the room.

Please, remember. Please, remember. She hoped he would. After all, they were natural born dance partners. That had to mean something.

When his gaze finally landed on her, a huge smile grew on his face. "Hey there."

"Robert!" she squealed, ran up the stairs, and stopped in front of him. She considered hugging him, but that would be odd. Warmth spread to her cheeks as she shuffled her feet. She had no idea what to say.

"Uh, do I know you?" he asked.

His smile faltered, and Lindsey's heart flopped.

"I'm Lindsey." She tried to stay happy, but it was hard.

Disappointment was nasty. It made her want to cry. "Come on. I'll show you the way out."

Taking his hand, she tugged him along behind her down the stairs, through the hole, and to the office door. Before opening it, she stopped.

It wasn't fair. She'd beaten the witch. She'd freed every single dancer. Couldn't she at least keep him as a friend?

Pushing a loose strand of hair out of her face, she forced determination. It probably wouldn't work, but she was going to try to get him to remember her. If he didn't, she was no worse off than before.

Not that the thought made her feel any better.

"We are...were friends. We danced *pas de deux*. You lifted me above your head. I was so scared you'd let me fall!"

"*Pas de huh?*" He laughed. "I don't dance. Try hockey. I'm a puck man through and through."

The way he threw his shoulders back and chest out irritated her. "A puck man? More like a bench warmer."

His smile disappeared. "Whatever." He reached out to push her to the side, but she held her ground.

"Please." She stared up at him, begging he'd listen to her. "Hold on one second, okay? I want to show you something. I promise, it's important."

Not waiting for an answer, she dashed back to the giant flower and snatched the amulet. The second she picked it up, the floating glitter disappeared, and the tulle petals pulled together. She jumped to the floor as the gigantic bud closed. Not wasting time, she spun around and bounded back to Robert, holding the amulet out in front of her.

"This belongs to you."

When he saw it, he let her give it to him. The moment it touched his skin, his eyes widened. "Whoa!" He grabbed his head with both of his hands as if he was trying to keep it from toppling off. "What happened? I feel as though I stepped off a rollercoaster."

"Do you remember me now?" she asked, carefully.

"Fuzzy bunny?" A teasing smile pulled at his lips.

151

"You remember!" It took everything she had not to grab him and squeeze him tight. "You know who I am!"

He rolled his eyes and laughed, but it cut short as he stared around the office. When he saw the hole with the room behind it, his face turned grim. "Where's Madame Destinée?"

"Gone."

He gazed down at her, confused. "What do you mean?"

Lindsey glanced at the broken music box on the floor. "I shrunk her in the machine. She's never coming back." She didn't want to explain the rest of the details. Not yet. She was too tired now.

"Well, I guess I should be getting back." He rubbed his hand through his hair and stared at his feet.

"Yeah, me, too." She shrugged, not knowing what to say.

Suddenly, he reached forward and pulled the amulet down over her head. "Here, it's yours. I gave it to you, remember? And don't you dare think of taking it off because I'm going to make sure you're wearing it the next time I see you."

"I'm going to see you again?" The biggest, widest, brightest smile formed on her lips. "You promise?"

"Well, you are my dance partner." His grin grew, making her heart grow with it. "But you're going to have to give me your address. If I'm going to have a dance partner, I've got to know where to find her."

Lindsey's heart pounded a thousand waltzes and more. "No problem, partner."

*H*olding Broussard in her arms, Lindsey pulled the door leading out of the dance school closed behind her and turned to the sidewalk to face the real world—New York, her home. The first cars of the morning rumbled by. A shop-keeper down the street groaned and huffed as he cranked out a worn red and white striped awning over the front of his store. It was so loud and busy, nothing like Nebraska. And that was great.

"Will you tell me the whole story again, the part about how the doggy helped you and the witch was trapped in the flower?" Bridget bounced up on top of the pile of ice along the side of the street.

"I've already told you everything."

"And? I want to hear it again!"

"Sure. But only one more time."

"Two more?" Bridget pleaded and bounced back down next to Lindsey.

Lindsey rolled her eyes. "Okay, two times, but no more."

She gazed back at Madame Destinée's dance school. The door was shut tight, and the windows were dark. It was time to walk away, but part of her didn't want to go. The building was magical, something special. If Madame Destinée hadn't been evil, her school would have been the most amazing thing in the world. Lindsey would have become a star. She might not dance again, but that was okay. She'd meant what she told Madame Destinée; nothing was more important than Bridget.

As sadness poked inside her chest, the building grew fuzzy around the edges. The dance school blurred, losing shape and form until it faded away. All that was left was a normal row of buildings and stores as if the school had never stood there at all.

"Magic," Lindsey whispered and scratched Broussard between the ears before handing him over to Bridget.

"He's so cute!" She cuddled him close to her chin.

As they rounded the corner with the hotdog stand, Lindsey pulled Bridget over to the pile of ice along the edge of the sidewalk. "Wait a second. I want to try something."

It was probably a bad idea, and she knew she'd kick herself for even trying, but something tugged inside of her to give it a go. Taking a deep breath, Lindsey darted along the top of the mound. Sure enough, her legs split at the right moment, and she flew over the ice in a more elegant jump than the one she'd performed days before. She almost biffed the landing, though. With her arms stretched out, she stood, accepting the applause and hoots from passersby, unable to believe what she'd done herself.

Everything Madame Destinée had said had been a lie.

Lindsey was talented, and that was something nobody could take away. Now, it was up to her to use and develop that talent as best as she could.

And she would. She'd be the best dancer the Community Center had ever seen and work her way up from there.

When Bridget and she arrived back home to the apartment building, Lindsey pushed the buzzer for Apartment 2A.

"That's not our apartment," Bridget complained.

"We have to visit Ms. Mulberry first." As a witch, Ms. Mulberry hopefully could make sure Mom and Dad remembered Bridget before Lindsey took her home. Otherwise, Bridget would be crushed, and she'd suffered enough as it was. Plus, Mom and Dad wouldn't hear the doorbell. Thanks to the little, metal music box, they should still be asleep.

Bridget crinkled her nose. "Is it because of the doggy?"

"No, because—"

Before she could say more, the door flew open. Instead of Ms. Mulberry, Mom and Dad appeared. They paused only for a breath before diving forward and picking both girls up into a gigantic bear hug.

"Mom! Dad!" Lindsey clung to them and held tight. The hypnotizing magic of the metal music box must have disappeared along with the rest of Madame Destinée's magic.

"Bridget! Lindsey! Where were you?" Lindsey's face squished so hard against Mom's stomach that she couldn't speak or breathe. But she smiled. Mom and Dad both remembered Bridget! That spell had disappeared, too.

When they finally let go, Bridget leaned over and whispered, "Are you going to tell them the whole story?"

Lindsey choked. The whole story? Mom and Dad would never believe it. But Bridget and she would have to come up with something. Maybe Ms. Mulberry would be of some help.

"I have an idea." She ruffled the fur on Broussard's head. "We'll let him take care of it."

THE END

About the Author

Tonja Drecker is a writer, blogger, children's book reviewer and freelance translator. After spending years in Germany exploring forgotten castles, she currently resides in the Ozarks with her family of six. When she's not tending her chickens and cows, she's discovering new adventures, nibbling chocolate and sipping a cup of tea.

www.tonjadreckerblogspot.com
www.facebook.com/TDrecker
www.twitter.com/TDrecker
www.bookwormforkids.blogspot.com

CPSIA information can be obtained
at www.ICGtesting.com
Printed in the USA
FFHW021147100219
50465225-55694FF